I0635645

# THE END OF THE BEGINNING

ENGEN

BOOKS

Published in Canada by Engen Books, St. John's, NL.

CIP information is available on Library and Archives Canada Cataloguing in Publication website.

ISBN-13: 978-1-77478-083-1

Copyright © 2022 Engen Books Ltd.

Cassidy Cane, Herbert Gamgee, and Tallis are copyright © 2022 by Matthew LeDrew.

The fictional worlds 'Alluvia' and 'Telluria' presented in this novella and all original characters and concepts presented thereon are copyright © 2022 by Amanda Labonté and Lauralana Dunne.

This book is a work of fiction. Names, characters, places and incidents are products of the author's imagination or are used fictitiously. Any resemblance to actual events or locales or persons living or dead is entirely coincidental.

NO PART OF THIS BOOK MAY BE REPRODUCED OR TRANSMITTED IN ANY FORM OR BY ANY MEANS, ELECTRONIC OR MECHANICAL, INCLUDING PHOTOCOPYING AND RECORDING, OR BY ANY INFORMATION STORAGE OR RETRIEVAL SYSTEM WITHOUT WRITTEN PERMISSION FROM THE AUTHOR, EXCEPT FOR BRIEF PASSAGES QUOTED IN A REVIEW.

Distributed by:
Engen Books
www.engenbooks.com
submissions@engenbooks.com

First mass market paperback printing: January 2022
Cover Design: Ellen Curtis
Slipstreamers Committee:
Amanda Labonté
Ali House
AJ Ryan
Ellen Curtis
Erin Vance
Lauralana Dunne
Matthew LeDrew

# THE UNEXPECTED VISITOR

## AMANDA LABONTÉ & JD RYOT

# CHAPTER ONE

Vacation. From the latin *vacare* meaning to be unoccupied.

It wasn't a term Cassidy Cane understood well. At least, not in practice. Dr. Gamgee, her mentor, had suggested a beach getaway. Somewhere sunny with sand and colourful drinks with little umbrellas.

Cassidy had quipped that she could hang out under an umbrella in her bomber jacket grading term papers and the doctor had laughed and laughed. Apparently, he'd been joking.

Instead, Cassidy found herself inside a cave, her only companion the soft sound of trickling water, as she stared at what to anyone else would appear to be an ordinary cave wall. But she knew it was anything but. Her instructions from Dr. Gamgee were to "try to have fun." Cassidy noted that he didn't tell her how to have fun. Which was just as well. She didn't have fun the way other people did, and she was perfectly fine with that.

Still, her family had started to worry about how hard she was working, so she'd convinced them she was spending a week at a Mexican resort with no cell service. It was a win-win situation. Her parents wouldn't worry about her, and she wouldn't have to check in. Giving her plenty of time for a little side adventure.

Cassidy pulled out a flashlight to do a last check of herself and her supplies, making certain she was ready for whatever waited for her on the other side. Or at least as ready as she could be. In addition to her practical clothing — her bomber jacket, sturdy boots, lightweight shirt and jeans, she also had a small backpack slung over her shoulder with essentials like batteries, protein bars, and water.

Her red hair was tied in a ponytail to keep it out of her way. A few locks fell forward as she looked down at her watch. It was just gone noon. The flight to Cancun would be readying for take-off. It was all clear for her own departure.

Go time.

Cassidy took a deep breath. No matter how many times she stepped through the portal, entering another world never got old. Her heart rate increased in anticipation and she stepped forward into, not a solid wall, but rather the disorienting pull of the portal. She felt a wave of warmth before emerging on the other side. It took only seconds for her to get her bearings — something she was getting better at.

First, she registered hard ground under her feet. For the briefest moment she thought she saw a flash of light, immediately to her right, but when she blinked again she was in complete darkness. Must have been a trick of her eyes. Emerging from a portal could do strange things to a body.

Rifling through her backpack, she found her flashlight

and got her first good look at where she'd landed. She was in a cave covered in shiny, glasslike rock, the kind that formed when magma cooled and hardened. She took quick stock of her surroundings. The cave was about ten feet wide — not huge, but more than enough room to maneuver. It appeared that — at least for the moment — she was by herself. That was always a good thing. She imagined that someday she might portal straight into a gathering again, but each time she emerged to find herself alone was a relief. Though, she smiled to herself at the thought of stumbling into a funeral, or worse, a wedding.

Cassidy picked up on the faint smell of vinegar as she approached the cave entrance. It wasn't difficult to breathe, but the smell definitely lingered. Maybe someone had been here recently, though she hoped it wasn't for a picnic. If the smell was indicative of their diet, she definitely wouldn't be staying long.

She made her way out of the cave opening and into a tunnel. The walls here were still shiny, though without the glow of the portal there was no natural light.

Checking her watch, Cassidy walked through the tunnel for a good twenty minutes and the only thing that changed was that the vinegary smell grew stronger. Finally, seeing daylight up ahead, she turned off the flashlight and walked out into the light — where her nostrils were immediately assaulted by the scent of rotting vegetation.

Combined with the vinegar, the smell was unpleasant enough that she thought about turning back and trying for another portal. Instead, she reached into her backpack and pulled out a blue scarf to tie around the lower half of her face.

The smell vaguely reminded her of a trip to Sao Paulo when air quality had been particularly poor from ozone pollution. Though the air in Sao Paulo had been vinegary and even a little earthy, it hadn't had that overwhelming rotten odour that had taken up residence in her nostrils.

How could anything with a sense of smell survive on a planet like this?

Having her scarf in place helped enough for Cassidy to get a decent look at her surroundings. Not that there was much to take in.

A desert of reddish sand spread out before her, like the sun in the dying atmosphere had been slowly baking the planet, leaving nothing but burned sand before her and a hulking mountain behind her.

The brownish sun dominated a yellowish sky that was likely the result of whatever pollutants were causing the planet's odour. It was too hazy to tell if there were clouds, but it definitely hadn't rained in days.

It didn't appear to have done anything in days.

Sure, she'd wanted a quiet adventure, but this was a bit too quiet. Ordinarily she would take a day or two to really explore a dead planet. She had enough snacks and water to last, but no way she could handle the smell that long.

Thinking that this might be the first time she turned around and left without any real observations, Cassidy decided to take one last, good look around. Opening her backpack again, she took out her binoculars. There was a mountain range in the distance, and she used that as her focal point. As she zeroed in, she realized they weren't mountains at all. It was a series of domes.

Being in a desert always messed with her perspective, but she was fairly certain the domes weren't that far away, maybe a couple of kilometres. It wasn't the most pleasant walk, but she'd managed worse.

She put the binoculars away, not wanting to leave them around her neck where they'd get in her way, and set out toward the nearest dome. In all likelihood she was heading toward the ruins of whatever civilization had once been here. At least she'd have something to show Dr. Gamgee from her "vacation."

She became more aware of the sun as she walked. It was hot, but not desert hot. At some point, the planet had likely had a fairly temperate climate.

As she approached the nearest dome — the one that appeared to be the largest, she could see that the structures were actually quite enormous — which explained how she'd mistaken it for a distant mountain range. She would be better able to confirm when she got closer, but the dome walls looked to be made of the same red-stained rock as the outside of the cave.

The walls went up quite high, arching overhead in a roof, making the structures akin to an igloo rather than a colosseum. The building of the dome was a feat that was comparable to earth's pyramids, though the pyramids had never been built to house this many people.

She wasn't sure how long she'd been walking when she realized that the shushing sound as her boots hitting the sand had become accompanied by a faint clicking noise. At first, she thought she'd imagined it — her brain was so used to filling in background noise like wind moving through plants or small insects buzzing — but there were no such noises here. Listening past the sound of her own feet, she heard it again.

*Click, click.*

Cassidy came to a stop. Silence. She took a couple steps forward.

*Click, click.*

She came to a halt. Silence.

This time when she moved, she counted her steps. One, two, three, four, five, *click, click.*

Something was monitoring her movements.

Her heart began to pound faster as she reached around for her backpack — intending to pull out her binoculars — when the ground beneath her feet shook and there was a scraping sound as a metal pole emerged from the ground. The pole was skinny, no bigger around than a chain link fence post and not much taller.

There was a low-pitched rustling sound, then the top of the post lit up with an orange flash that was accompanied by a woman's voice. As she spoke, the light blinked on and off with her words.

"Unexpected visitor, you are entering the Alluvian military compound. Please await an escort."

"Hello?" Cassidy called. She took a step forward, but the message repeated itself at a slightly higher volume.

*So it's a recording, but it can sense movement,* she thought to herself.

A whirring noise pulled her attention back toward the dome. Something was heading in her direction.

She pulled out her binoculars, spilling a couple of granola bars in her haste, and held the lenses up to her eyes. A black vehicle was headed in her direction. It vaguely resembled a hummer, in that it was hulking and able to manoeuver in the desert, but there were major differences. There were no windows, and she couldn't make out any doors along the sides.

As it drew closer, she stuffed the binoculars in her bag and crouched down to pick up the granola bars she'd dropped. Apparently, the sensors took the movement as an attempt to flee the scene.

"Unexpected guest, do not attempt to leave. Await escort."

Cassidy straightened. The transport was close enough that she could make out its shape without the need for binoculars. Unlike earth cars, the front was flat, and windowless like the rest of the vehicle. The driver must have had an alternate means of seeing the terrain.

She also noticed that the vehicle moved with stealth. While the talking light pole had shaken the ground, the massive alien hummer barely emitted any noise. It had to be a much more advanced technology.

Which made no sense. Why on earth would a civilization not keep their surveillance systems up to date?

The hulking black vehicle came to a stop a few feet away from the flashing post and Cassidy looked back to the orange light, half expecting it to give her further instructions, but instead, she heard a smooth whirring noise and an armored figure — also in black — unfolded itself from the back of the vehicle in the approximate location that a spare tire would be kept on an earth SUV.

"That looks like a really uncomfortable way to travel," Cassidy said as the figure straightened to its full height of about six feet. She wasn't sure if there was a sentient being inside the armor or if it was some kind of robot. The arms and legs were too skinny for a human to be inside, but there was no guarantee the other beings on the planet would appear humanoid.

The bulb-shaped head did not rotate in her direction, which either meant that the being inside did not need to turn its head to see, or it was some kind of AI that used sensors. The helmet lit up with an orange light as the being began to speak.

"Unexpected visitor, this is your escort to the Alluvian military compound."

A door swung open in the front of the vehicle revealing bench seating on each side.

"No driver then," Cassidy said to herself as stepped into the vehicle. The door swung shut behind her, plunging her into darkness.

# CHAPTER TWO

It occurred to Cassidy that perhaps she was walking straight into danger, but she dismissed the thought. No one had threatened her outright and she was quite curious to discover the kind of civilization lived on what appeared to be a dead planet.

She assumed they were headed into one of the domes, but it would have been nice to have a window. There was a ceiling light that gave off an orange glow, illuminating the black interior. The bench seat she sat on was made of a foam-like material that was comfortable enough and the floor and ceiling were black metal. It was all very utilitarian.

At least the air in the vehicle was better than what was outside. Cassidy appreciated the ventilation system and the smooth ride.

Checking her watch, Cassidy saw that she'd been inside less than five minutes when she felt the vehicle slow. Her assumption that they were bringing her to the nearest dome seemed correct.

The vehicle came to a complete stop and she heard a gentle hissing sound as the door opened. Cassidy was ready to push herself off the bench when a face with color-less eyes appeared in the doorway.

The being was remarkably humanoid in appearance, though their skin was so pale that Cassidy wouldn't have been surprised to find that it was translucent.

*That answers the question about the being on the back of the vehicle,* Cassidy thought as she looked over the individual in front of her once more, taking in human arms and legs. *Definitely a robot.*

"We mean you no harm," the being said in a feminine sounding voice. "I'm Officer Elona."

Elona wore a suit of brick-red and her hair was pulled back, covered by a black cap. Her face was smooth, expression unreadable.

"I'm Cassidy Cane."

Elona stepped back, giving Cassidy space to step out of the vehicle. Once she was outside, Cassidy could see she was in a well-lit, cave-like area with red stone walls. There was a set of large metal doors behind her, presumably where the vehicle had entered. In front of her, behind Elona, was another doorway, a smaller one that had been left open. Though Cassidy couldn't see much, she thought it led into a hallway.

If she had to guess, she would put herself just inside a dome's entrance.

But the thing that really caught her attention was the air. The smell was gone.

"I didn't mean to intrude," Cassidy said, untying her scarf and taking a deep breath. She noticed that the air in the cave was thinner. It felt like she was breathing at the top of a mountain.

Still, it was much fresher than what she'd experienced outside.

"We don't get visitors here," Elona said. "Forgive our lack of protocols, but we're doing our best under the circumstances."

"No apology necessary," Cassidy said as the door to the vehicle closed behind her.

"I have instructions to bring you to the captain," Elona said. "Follow me."

Cassidy had definitely had more abrupt first encounters. As she followed Elona into a hallway, a metal door closed behind them, sealing them off from the entrance cave. A light panel next to the door lit up in blue. She took a quick inventory of her surroundings as they walked down the hallway. Again, the walls were red stone. The light source was definitely artificial, but it was soft, with a yellow tinge like a sunny day.

Up close, she could see that Elona's skin wasn't actually white. There was a definite pinkish tinge to it. Similarly, her eyes weren't actually colourless. There was a pale purple in the irises.

Cassidy caught a glimpse of a lock of hair that had come loose from under her cap. Unlike the rest of her, Elona's hair was a vibrant fuchsia.

A multitude of questions raced through Cassidy's head as she walked. Many had to do with Elona herself. How old was she? What kind of officer was she? But Cassidy didn't know if those questions would seem too forward. After all, she knew nothing of their customs.

She decided instead to stick to more general questions.

"What's up with this planet?"

Elona glanced at her. "Where did you come from?"

"You first," Cassidy said, forcing a smile. She needed more time to organize her backstory. She couldn't tell them about the portals, so she'd need a cover. Would these people be freaked out by space travel? So far, they seemed to be dealing quite well with her alien presence.

Though, that could all change on a dime.

"Our planet became toxic many centuries back," Elona explained. "We created these domes to preserve our people from the worst effects of the polluted air."

"And you filter the air inside?"

"Yes," Elona answered. She shrugged her shoulders once and Cassidy wondered if that was the earth equivalent of nodding your head. She made a mental note to watch for the gesture.

"This is our main base," Elona said as they emerged into a large, round courtyard. The walls went up so high, Cassidy couldn't make out the ceiling. She could see window-like openings though, they were spaced out evenly in the red stone walls and rose up at least six or seven storeys.

The stone inside was a lighter, more yellowy orange than the red stone outside the dome. Just like in the cave, there was a light source that mimicked a sunny day.

There were tables set out, as well as a counter serving what Cassidy assumed was this planet's equivalent of coffee. A few people dressed in the same red uniform as Elona sat at the tables in groups of two or three. None looked directly their way, but Cassidy sensed that they were being observed, mainly by the fact that there was absolutely no conversation at any of the tables.

"The captain would like to meet us in the formal garden," Elona said as they continued through the courtyard and out into another hallway, though this one was much shorter. They emerged in another round space with a number of trees, all with thin, white trunks. The heart-shaped leaves had the faintest tinge of colour with shades yellow, purple and green around their edges. It was as though a vampire had sucked nearly all of the life out of the plants.

The lack of colour reminded her of Elona's skin.

"These are beautiful." Cassidy reached out to touch a pale gold leaf and it disintegrated in her hand like ancient parchment.

"Our plants are quite fragile," Elona explained.

"I'm sorry."

Elona shrugged once and led her more fully into the space. They emerged from the trees to find three figures standing before them.

The person in the middle was the tallest and his uniform had the most patches. At a guess, Cassidy assumed this was the captain. To his right was a female who wore a red lab coat and no hat on her head of deep green hair. The trio was rounded out by a young man who was also in uniform.

"Welcome to Alluvia," the man in the middle took a step forward. Cassidy caught a glimpse of blue under his cap. His irises and skin were also tinged blue. "I'm Captain Kruz, the officer in charge of this military base."

"It's nice to meet you," Cassidy said. "I'm Cassidy Cane."

"She looks almost Tellurian," the male to the captain's left said. "Though, her colouring is a bit off."

"That's enough, Lupo," Captain Kruz said. "Cassidy is our guest."

Her name came out as 'Ka-si-dee' in the Captain's accent. She noted that they elongated their 'Es' but shortened the consonants. She wanted to know what a Tellurian was. The way everyone reacted made her think it was an insult. Before she got a chance to ask for clarification, the woman in the red jacket spoke up.

"I would like to run some tests," she said. "The fact that she can breathe on our planet is...remarkable."

The last thing Cassidy wanted was to be poked and prodded, but she wasn't sure if she actually had a choice. These beings seemed quite nice, but that didn't mean they wouldn't use force.

At her hesitation, the woman took a step forward. "I assure you, our tests are quite advanced. There will be no pain."

"Dr. Arasellie is our best medic," Captain Kruz assured her.

"Just the same, I'd rather not have my DNA harvested by another race," Cassidy said.

Rather than get defensive, the doctor shrugged once. "I understand your reticence. I can assure you that I am only interested in your lungs."

"My lungs?" Cassidy looked from the doctor to the captain. Neither of them so much as blinked — as though they didn't want to spook her. "You aren't going to remove them from my body, right? You just want to have a listen?"

A small smile tugged at Dr. Arasellie's lips. "I will not. What's more, I won't perform any tests without explaining first."

"Why my lungs?"

"Isn't it obvious?" Lupo spoke up. "We can't breathe the outside air."

While some body language was open to interpretation, Cassidy didn't need any special observation skills to decipher the glare Captain Kruz was aiming at Lupo. Cassidy noted that, like the captain, Lupo had blue tinged skin. Perhaps the two males were related. It would explain why the captain had him at his side despite the young man's obvious incompetence.

"A basic scan of your lungs might give us some insight that could help us in dealing with our own diseases," Dr. Arasellie said. "It would be purely observational."

"I can understand that," Cassidy said, and it was the truth. She was always spending her time looking for medical answers, maybe this was her chance to give back a little.

Besides, she'd never met an alien lab she hadn't wanted to explore.

# CHAPTER THREE

Cassidy was left in the care of Dr. Arasellie and Elona, presumably while Captain Kruz went off to reprimand Lupo and take the Alluvian equivalent of a couple of aspirin.

Dr. Arasellie was much chattier than Elona and Cassidy chalked it up to the differences between being an officer and being a scientist. If the tables were turned, Cassidy definitely would take the opportunity to carry on a full conversation with an alien.

They moved from the formal garden into another short hallway that led to an even larger dome, this one crowded with people, moving between what appeared to be stalls.

"Is this a market?" Cassidy asked, coming to a stop and nearly colliding with a male in a short sleeve button-down in a shade of deep blue. He didn't spare Cassidy a glance as he rushed to a stall with a table set out with different sized screens.

Standing on her tiptoes, Cassidy could see several of the vendors. A few sold food, though she wasn't close enough to really see more than the shape of bread on a plate. There was also a clothing booth with shirts and pants in a rainbow of colors. But the most popular stalls were those selling electronics. She saw the blue shirted man sticking something in his ear before picking up a screen to test out.

It was such an interesting combination of an old-fashioned market mixed with a modern society, that Cassidy hadn't realized Dr. Arasellie had completely disappeared into the crowd. Fortunately, Elona was still at her side.

"This way," she said, leading Cassidy out of the market and into another hallway.

"How many domes are there?" Cassidy asked.

Elona thought for a moment. "In the military complex, you mean? Twenty-seven."

"How about the whole planet?"

"I'd have to check."

Cassidy thought back to her observations outside with her binoculars. "That's a lot of domes."

"Only a few are large. There's the market and the atrium, which you've seen. And, of course, the animal pasture which we'll pass soon."

"Animal pasture?" Cassidy asked as they caught up with Dr. Arasellie.

"There you are, I thought we'd lost you in the market. Right this way."

Cassidy followed the doctor through a short hallway and emerged into a brightly lit dome with large fluffy white creatures scattered all about. They reminded her of cows crossed with sheep.

There was the faint smell of manure, but given the closed space and the number of animals, it should have been overpowering.

"Why doesn't it smell worse?" Cassidy asked.

Doctor Arasellie's lips pulled up at the corners. "That's thanks to our ventilation system. Evidently it must be quite good if you've noticed it?"

"Quite," Cassidy agreed.

Dr. Arasellie stopped near one of the fuzzy cows. "These are vecas."

"Are they a food source?" Cassidy asked. "I assume growing crops is difficult."

"Impossible," the doctor agreed. "You saw the state of the trees in the formal garden."

Cassidy remembered how the leaves had fallen apart in her fingers.

"The lab is just up here," Dr. Arasellie said, moving away from the vecas and leading them into another hallway, but instead of emerging into yet another dome, they turned into a doorway that led to an open-air shaft that turned out to be an elevator. There were no sliding doors or light up buttons, it was far more basic, just a scuffed-up metal platform, a railing with cables attached to it and a series of levers. As they stepped onto the platform, Dr. Arasellie pulled the third lever and they rose more smoothly than Cassidy would have thought possible.

They ascended from the ground floor up two storeys before coming to an easy stop. Dr. Arasellie disembarked first but Elona waited for Cassidy to step off before following. It was a subtle reminder that, as nice as her companions were, Cassidy wasn't free to move about on her own.

"Here we are," Dr. Arasellie stopped in front of a glass door. She typed in a code and the door slid open.

Like the other spaces she had seen, the walls and floor of the lab were yellowish stone. There was a window on the wall opposite the door and Cassidy could see the vecas grazing below. It was almost like looking out over an open field.

Even with the artificial lighting, the lab still had a cave-like quality that was juxtaposed with the modern equipment that dominated the room. There was a large tube that was much like a microscope that dominated one table and monitors sat atop desks, their screens lit up in various colors that could have been a simple screen saver, or evidence the machine was performing a complex analysis.

"If it's all right with you, I'd like to start by taking a picture of your lungs," Dr. Arasellie said, leading her to a round booth in the corner of the room. "Just step in here and try not to move."

Assuming it was the Alluvian version of an x-ray, Cassidy stepped inside while Dr. Aradellie played with the control panel.

"Do I need to take off my jacket or anything?"

Dr. Arasellie laughed. "Why would you need to do that? Just stand as straight as possible, it'll only take a few seconds."

Elona was less interested in the medical procedures and had wandered over to the window.

"We should be just about done," Dr. Aradellie said. Cassidy looked at her in surprise.

"So quick?"

The doctor shrugged. "Come this way and I'll show you."

Cassidy stepped out of the booth and followed Dr.

Arasellie to a monitor with an oval shaped keyboard. As she typed, the screen went from shapes shifting in no distinctive pattern to slowly creating a clear picture of the organs inside her body.

"So much color," Dr. Arasellie said in an awed voice. "So healthy."

"Thanks." Cassidy said. "But I don't understand why you're so impressed."

Dr. Arasellie turned back to the keyboard and typed in a series of commands. The image on the screen shifted to show a different set of lungs. These were a blush color.

"These are a typical Alluvian's lungs. That is, an Alluvian in peak condition."

"You mean a healthy Alluvian?"

Dr. Arasellie shook her head. "None of us are healthy, not truly, but with proper treatment we can survive childhood."

Cassidy's stomach muscles clenched. "What sort of treatment?"

Dr. Arasellie returned to the keyboard and this time the image that appeared was of a small set of opalescent lungs.

"These belong to a typical child on our planet. With proper medication and high doses of vitamin D, many children will develop enough lung strength to grow to adulthood."

Cassidy swallowed hard. "No wonder you wanted to see my lungs."

Dr. Arasellie shrugged once. "This lab is one of many devoted to lung studies, though, being on the military complex means I have access to the best resources."

"Do you run tests here?"

"Yes, would you like to see?"

Dr. Arasellie's fingers flew across the keys showing Cassidy all kinds of diseases and test results.

"Wait." Cassidy pointed at the screen where Dr. Arasellie was showing off a test for detecting early growths. "How does this work?"

"This one? That's a simple blood exam."

A simple blood exam that detected early lung cancer. Cassidy could feel the adrenaline pumping through her veins. This would be a game changer for so many people on earth.

"It's nearly mealtime," Elona said, stepping away from the window. Cassidy had almost forgotten the officer was still with them. "The captain has invited you to dine with him."

"We can speak again," Dr. Arasellie said, as though she could sense Cassidy's hesitation.

"I'd like that," Cassidy said, before turning her attention to Elona. "Where are we going now?"

"I thought you'd like to change for dinner," Elona said. "I've arranged for you to borrow some clothes."

Cassidy glanced down at her jacket. "Is there something wrong with what I'm wearing?"

"You smell," Elona said. "You have ever since you arrived."

# CHAPTER FOUR

Cassidy wasn't only given a change of clothes, but also a room to shower in. Or, at least what the Alluvians did as a shower. It was more of a dry-cleaning cell, but it did the trick. Her clothes were being similarly cleaned, but it was apparently going to take some time to get the smell of the planet's atmosphere out of her jacket. Now that she was in clean clothes herself, she could appreciate Elona's manners in not saying something sooner.

The clothing was much like what she'd seen in the market earlier that day, a button-down shirt in a vibrant shade of blue with matching pants. Both were of a linen material that was lightweight and warm.

The room she'd been assigned was small, like a dorm room, though it did have its own bathroom, which was a relief. The sleeping area resembled a shelf with a palette built into the wall. The room was laid out to make as much use of the limited floor area as possible.

There was one small window that looked out on the courtyard Cassidy had seen the officers sitting in upon her arrival, though she was up high enough that she couldn't really get a good view of the happenings below.

Fixing her hair into a braid, Cassidy sat on the chair under the bed shelf and waited for Elona to return. She tried not to stress about the fact that the dorm door had locked shut behind her.

They wouldn't have given her nice clothes if she was a prisoner.

Cassidy was starting to second guess herself for trusting these people when the panel on the wall next to her door shifted from blue to yellow and Elona entered.

"You are ready?" Elona asked, looking over Cassidy's blue outfit. Cassidy noticed that Elona had also changed, though she still wore a red uniform. This one appeared more comfortable, made of a similar material to what Cassidy was wearing.

"All ready," Cassidy agreed. She'd nodded once or twice but noted that the Alluvians didn't appear to understand the motion. She'd made a mental note to answer every question out loud.

Elona led her out into a hallway and to the open-air elevator they'd used earlier. The dorm room was about five storeys up and Cassidy held on as they went straight down to the bottom floor.

When they stepped out of the elevator, Elona led her out to the courtyard, which she could see had been somewhat transformed from earlier that day. The small cafe style tables had been moved, and were replaced by one large round table.

There were a few Alluvians standing around, no more than a dozen, mostly dressed in red. Cassidy recognized Dr. Arasellie and Lupo, alongside Captain Kruz, who was also joined by a woman in a jade green tunic dress that set off her yellow gold hair.

At her arrival, the captain and the woman in green stepped forward. Up close, Cassidy could see that the woman's skin also had a yellow cast to it — not like human jaundice, more like sunshine.

She was stunning.

"Cassidy," Kruz said with a shoulder shrug. "This is my wife, Mirta."

"Nice to meet you."

Mirta smiled. "When my husband told me we had an unexpected visitor, I assumed the worst."

"Really?" Cassidy's curiosity was piqued. "Who were you expecting?"

"I believe dinner is ready," Kruz said, cutting off his wife's answer. "Better to talk over food."

Cassidy was led to the seat between the captain and Dr. Araisellie. Elona and Lupo had the seats furthest from her, right across from her at the large round table. The seats in between were taken by soldiers with varying numbers of patches on their uniforms and Cassidy guessed they were seated closest to the captain according to rank.

Which made her the guest of honor.

The place setting in front of Cassidy was made up of an earthy red clay plate and metal utensils. The cup was made of the same pottery as the plate but was shaped more like a drinking glass.

A pair of servers dressed in black linen entered carrying trays. They placed a round roll of bread, a serving of meat and a salad of blue-tinged leaves on Cassidy's plate. She waited until everyone was served before asking about the food.

"What kind of vegetable is this?" She picked up a leaf.

"That's chuga, it's vital to our diet."

Cassidy noted that everyone around her had already started eating, all starting with the vegetables. She picked up a forkful and began chewing. It tasted like really bad spinach, but the Alluvians appeared to love it.

"Where do you grow it?" Cassidy asked. She'd seen the vecas, which explained the meat source, but not the vegetation. At her question, the table grew still, and Cassidy wondered if she'd made a faux-pas. Finally, Captain Kruz answered.

"All our grown food comes from Telluria, a nearby moon."

The word sounded familiar, and Cassidy remembered Lupo's comment from earlier in the day, about her looking Tellurian.

"So, you have an arrangement with the Tellurians?" Cassidy asked.

"It's hardly an arrangement," Mirta said, the anger seeping through her voice. "They hardly give us enough to survive."

"I don't understand." Cassidy looked around the table. She could admit that the Alluvians looked fragile, likely due to their weaker lungs, but she hadn't seen the tell-tale signs of a civilization on the brink of starvation.

"It's the chuga," Dr. Arasellie explained. "It's filled with vitamin D, which is essential to lung development, especially in our children. Without it, we cannot survive."

"That's...awful," Cassidy said, staring down at the

wilted leaves on her plate. She wanted to scrape it off onto the Alluvian plates around her, but she didn't know enough about their culture to know if that would be mortally offensive or not.

Instead, she ate it so she could move on to the bread and meat.

"It's a constant source of strain between ourselves and the Tellurians," Captain Kruz said. "We only want enough for the survival of our children."

A server came around with a jug of thick, green juice and filled their glasses, but Cassidy noticed that no one drank while they ate.

"Even the Tellurian moon isn't the most stable growing environment," Dr. Arasellie said, continuing where the captain had left off. "We grow a special fertilizer in our labs that helps them grow all their food."

"And in exchange, all we ask is that they give us a proper allotment of chuga," Mirta added.

"Have you considered leaving your planet?" Cassidy asked as she tore the roll in half. The bread also had a blue tinge, but it tasted pretty good, much better than the chuga. "Surely with your technology you could find another planet or moon to inhabit."

"Unfortunately, that is not possible for us," Dr. Arasellie said. "While we have the technology, we don't have the means to survive on another planet. On any planet, really."

"Because of your breathing?"

"It makes travel impossible. All our shipments to and from Telluria are managed through artificial intelligence pilots."

"That's fascinating," Cassidy said, finishing up her meat. She noted that most everyone else was already done eating.

"Indeed," Captain Kruz said. "And now that you've had some time to learn about us, I think it's time to learn about you, Cassidy Cane. Where do you come from? And how did you get here?"

# CHAPTER FIVE

She'd known this was coming, and she was grateful to have been able to gather as much information as she had before they'd started really asking questions. Knowing that the Alluvians couldn't leave their domes meant that she could easily hide the fact that she'd arrived by portal.

"I'm sure you have your own theories?" Cassidy said, chewing the last of her bread. "I can't be your first visitor?"

There had, afterall, been a surveillance system in place, as archaic as it had first appeared.

"It has been some time," Captain Kruz said. "We are not on the usual path of explorers."

"I assumed as much," Cassidy said, hoping no one called her bluff. "I was surprised to see the planet on my navigation system."

"Did your ship crash?" Lupo called from the across the table.

"No, but I needed to make a landing to make some minor repairs, which was when I decided to go for a walk."

"And lucky for us you did," Mirta said. "Your presence has been most fortuitous."

Cassidy wanted to clarify what Mirta meant, but at that moment there was a minor commotion and a small girl with Mirta's gold hair came tearing into the courtyard. She was followed closely by a harried-looking male with powder blue hair.

"Apologies," the male said as the girl came to a stop next to the captain and attempted to climb into his lap. "But she got away from me."

"Trica, what have you been told about running away from your nurse?"

The small girl didn't pay the captain any attention, instead she focused her bright blue eyes on Cassidy.

"Is that her, Papa? Is that the girl who can breathe outside?"

Cassidy looked from Trica to the captain, unsure how to respond.

"I think this is a good time to clear the table," Mirta said, gesturing for the servers to return.

As they rose from the table, Cassidy noted that the other guests took their cups with them, so she did the same as she stepped back from the table.

"Please forgive my daughter," Captain Kruz said, coming to stand next to Cassidy while his wife stayed across the room with Trica and the nurse. The little girl appeared to be in no hurry to leave.

"She's sweet," Cassidy said, watching as the little girl stared at her while talking animatedly to her mother. She realized she was looking at a child who'd never felt the sun or the wind. "How long have you lived like this?"

Captain Kruz sipped his drink and Cassidy brought her own cup to her lips and took a tentative taste. It was thick, but also quite sweet. All in all, not too bad.

"I think it's time I brought you to our gallery."

Only the Captain, Elona and Lugo accompanied her to the gallery. She didn't mind hanging out with the captain and Elona, but she would have liked to leave Lugo back in the courtyard. He wasn't intentionally rude, but the way he looked at her made Cassidy think he saw her as an interesting specimen rather than a rational being.

They didn't have to go to a different dome, but they did have to take the elevator all the way to the top. Upon arrival, they exited the lift and rather than a series of doors and rooms, this floor was one continuous hallway with round windows lining one side and large works of art lining the other.

"This is my favorite place," Elona said, taking a step toward the closest picture. It was large, about a meter high and a meter and half wide. Cassidy stopped next to Elona to better take in the piece. As she got closer, she realized it wasn't a painting, but rather a digital representation on a monitor.

The image was a mountain landscape, much like the one she'd seen outside the dome, though this one was covered in plantlife — vegetation in pinks, greens and yellows.

"This was Alluvia," Captain Kruz said, "before the planet died."

"It's beautiful," Cassidy said, wishing she could have seen it at its peak. "What happened?"

"Pollution, overuse of resources that deteriorated the atmosphere."

"How long ago was this?"

"About a thousand years."

Cassidy knew she was doing a poor job of hiding her shock. "You've been living indoors for a millennium?"

Rather than answer, Captain Kruz moved on to the next picture. Both Elona and Lugo hung back.

This time the image included people. They all had the same brightly colored hair as the Alluvians Cassidy had met, but their skin was a much deeper color. All kinds of shades from reds and pinks to blues and greens. There were even browns and creams.

"This is how we used to look," Captain Kruz said. "But after years away from the sun and fresh air, we've lost much of our color."

Based on the images Dr. Arasellie had shown her, Cassidy knew this wasn't only the case on the outside, but also on the inside as well.

The next image was of another planet as seen from space.

"That's Telluria," Captain Kruz said. "Our moon."

"Who lives there?" Cassidy asked.

"Tellurians," Lugo said the word like it left a bad taste in his mouth. He was a few steps behind, but obviously had overheard her question.

"And they're a separate race?" Cassidy directed her question to the captain.

"They are now. But we used to live here together. A group of Alluvians were sent to the moon when it was clear the planet could no longer sustain us."

The next image bore out Captain Kruz's story. It was a ship arriving on a moon covered in spiky green vegetation. All the people in the picture had the deep skin tones of the Alluvians in the previous picture.

It was no wonder Lugo had said she looked Tellurian. Her skin tone would almost blend in.

"This is the point where our two races split apart," Captain Kruz said. "We became Alluvians and Tellurians."

"I know Alluvians can't leave this planet, but don't the Tellurians ever come back down?"

Surely the two races could have continued to co-mingle?

"Never," Lugo said. "We'd never let them set foot here."

"That's enough," Captain Kruz reprimanded the young officer before turning back to Cassidy. "We can't risk the Tellurians coming back here. They could decimate us so easily."

"Because of your health?"

Captain Kruz shrugged. "If they knew how fragile we were, what would stop them from stealing our technology and letting us perish? We'd have no way to fight them off outside our dome. Our separation is the only thing that protects us."

The captain continued walking. The next image showed pale Alluvians surrounding half-built domes.

"The collapse of our atmosphere nearly eliminated us. For centuries our birth-rate fell, and our life expectancy was short. It is only thanks to our ever-advancing technology and research in diet and supplements that we are finally able to rebuild our population."

"But your children still have a difficult time reaching

adulthood?"

"Yes, they require high volumes of a vitamin D enriched diet. Some more than others. Unfortunately, the Tellurians refuse to grow an adequate supply of chuga, which means we have to ration as best we can. For many children, that won't be enough."

The captain didn't have to say anything — she knew his daughter was one of those who might not make it.

# CHAPTER SIX

It took Cassidy several seconds to orient herself when she woke up the next morning.

She'd had a surprisingly restful sleep on the shelf bed and had woken up with an idea.

But first things first, she needed her own clothes back.

Carefully climbing off the bed, she went to look out the window. She'd learned the night before that the lights inside the dome were controlled to mimic day and night and all the lighting changes in between.

Looking out now, she could easily convince herself that early morning sunlight was streaming in.

She turned back to her room and went to the wall-mounted device that worked like a dry-cleaner but opened like an oven. She pulled down the door and took out her jacket and held it up to her nose.

It smelled like honey and sage. A vast improvement.

Cassidy prepared for the day, even getting another dry shower, and dressed in her own clothes. Then she went to the panel by the door and entered the code Elona had given her, making the light change from blue to green. The door didn't open, but it did send a message to let Elona know she wanted to leave.

Cassidy paced the small space and reminded herself that she wasn't a prisoner — the Alluvians had no reason to trust and, in fact, had been remarkably kind.

The door slid open and Elona stood outside holding a tray.

"I thought you might be hungry," she said.

There were two dishes on the tray: a bowl of something that looked like a pale blue oatmeal, and another chuga salad. Cassidy looked at the tray and then back to Elona. She pointed at the oatmeal.

"I'll eat that, but I would prefer it if you ate the chuga."

Elona frowned. "Is it not to your liking?"

"It's not that, it's more that I don't need it. There's too much vitamin D in it for me."

Elona tilted her head as she observed Cassidy. "No one is supposed to eat outside their ration."

"Not even to prevent waste?"

The other girl thought for a moment. "If the chuga were to be wasted, it is acceptable for anyone to eat it. But only under those circumstances."

"Well then, you'd better come in and prevent some wastage."

While they ate, Cassidy decided to ask about going back to the lab.

"Dr. Arasellie would be pleased to see you again," Elona said, finishing up the last of the lettuce. "Would you like to go there now?"

"Yes, unless there's something else you wanted to

do?"

"Captain Kruz thought you might like to see our other labs."

"Actually, that does sound like fun."

Elona shrugged once. "We can visit Dr. Arasellie on our way back, if you wish?"

"Yes, thank you."

The other labs were in a completely new area, past the dome where the vecas roamed.

"What's in there?" Cassidy pointed at a set of metal doors as they went down a new hallway.

"That's the hangar where our ships land with the rations from Telluria."

"Do shipments arrive often?"

"It depends on the time of year. We're in the growing season, so it's more frequent at this time."

Elona led her further down the hallway to an open-air shaft where they took the lift to the top. Like the gallery Captain Kruz had taken her to, it was an open concept area but that's where the similarities with the other space ended. This was definitely a lab. All the surfaces — aside from the walls and floors — were black and shiny and there was a faint chemical smell in the air.

"This is where the fertilizer is grown," Elona explained as she led Cassidy fully into the space.

Unlike Dr. Arasellie's lab, this one bustled with people. They all wore lab coats in varying shades of orange and red and seemed busy looking through microscopes or setting up samples in petri style dishes.

"Professor Malen?"

Upon hearing his name, a male with pink hair in a

clashing brick red lab coat broke off from a group and approached them.

"Officer, I'd been told to expect you and our visitor." Professor Malen gave them a tight smile and his posture was stiff.

"Thank you for agreeing to show your lab," Cassidy said. "I hope I'm not intruding?"

"We're in our busy season," the professor said. "But I can take a few minutes to give a tour."

Cassidy followed the professor into the very centre of the space where he directed her gaze up.

Above them was a glass ceiling covered in pots overflowing with a bluish, algae-like substance. But it wasn't the plant-life that caught Cassidy's attention, it was the light source.

"Is that the sun?"

"Yes," Professor Malen said. "It's filtered so that the toxicity doesn't affect the fertilizer."

While she watched, two scientists helped a third get into a suit that strongly resembled very old earth scuba diving equipment, complete with a round helmet that had an air hose coming out the top, attached to a tank on her back. Once the gear was secure, the scientist climbed a ladder and opened a trap door in a part of the ceiling with no plants. It took Cassidy a moment to see the glass wall that divided the plant area from the trapdoor.

Once the scientist was completely through, she closed the trap door and opened another in the wall leading to the plants.

*It's an airlock,* Cassidy thought, as she watched the scientist move plants from one part of the ceiling to the other. The air filtering in with the sunlight must have been toxic enough that it wasn't safe for the scientists to breathe even in small doses.

When the scientist finished moving plants, she returned to the airlock and closed the door behind her before opening the trapdoor and handing the pots down to the scientists waiting on the ladder. They all wore gloves and cloth face coverings.

"This fertilizer will be shipped to Telluria where it will help grow vegetation," Professor Malen explained.

"Like chuga?"

The professor shrugged once. "Among other things."

They stayed another few minutes; and Cassidy watched as several scientists packed the algae fertilizer into crates, keeping gloves on the entire time.

"Did you still want to see Dr. Arasellie?" Elona asked.

"Yes, if that's possible?"

"Of course," Elona said. They went back to the lift but went down three floors — stopping so that Elona could check in with her supervising officer before they continued on.

"If you don't mind waiting here, I'll be back momentarily," Elona said, leaving Cassidy in the hallway outside the office.

Cassidy leaned against the wall, going over plans in her head for how she'd talk to Dr. Arasellie and for what exactly she could offer.

When several minutes passed without Elona's return, Cassidy became restless. Unlike the other floors she'd been on, the offices on this floor were built against the outside of the dome, which meant they must not have had any windows at all.

Cassidy looked up and down the hallway and saw there was one small window further down. She headed for it and was disappointed to see that there was nothing but darkness on the other side.

Remembering the steel doors, Cassidy reached into her backpack and took out her flashlight. She was only one floor up from the bottom, not too far for her beam to catch something.

She shone the light into the darkness and hit off...a ship?

The beam travelled around a hull. Definitely a ship.

Cassidy wished she had a better source of light. There was definitely something familiar about the ship. It looked like the one in the picture she'd seen in the gallery — the one that had brought the Tellurians to their moon.

But if that were the case, why was it back here?

Cassidy heard footsteps and turned off her light, cramming it in her backpack.

"There you are," Elona said. "Are you ready to see Dr. Arasellie?"

"Yes, of course. Lead the way."

# CHAPTER SEVEN

Dr. Arasellie appeared pleased to see her. At the very least her smile wasn't as forced as Professor Malen's had been, though they did have to wait for her to finish an appointment.

Upon their arrival, the doctor had two small children in her lab. Cassidy figured they were twins, based on their matching blue curls and similar height.

"Is that the unexpected visitor?" One of the children asked, pointing at Cassidy.

"That's her," Dr. Arasellie said. "Now, let's get you back to your nurse."

The children grumbled, wanting to stay behind to see the alien, but Dr. Arasellie shooed them out the door. Cassidy smiled and waved as they walked past and their eyes grew round, though one of them waved back and even gave her a shy smile.

Once the children were settled, Dr. Arasellie returned to the lab.

"I hope I'm not disrupting?" Cassidy asked. "I should have realized you'd have patients to see. Do you see a lot of children?"

"Unfortunately, I see mainly children."

Cassidy's stomach clenched. "Will those twins be ok?"

Dr. Arasellie didn't answer immediately, choosing her words. "I think at least one of them will be."

Cassidy tried to find words but couldn't. She noticed that the picture of her lungs was up on the screen alongside the pale image of those belonging to an Alluvian child.

"Why don't you tell me what brings you by?" Dr. Arasellie asked. "Your timing is excellent, as I have a bit of break."

"Actually, I was wondering if I might be of some use to you," Cassidy said. "I was thinking we could do a kind of information exchange."

"An exchange?" The doctor tilted her head to one side, looking Cassidy over from boots to nose. "What information could you possibly need from us?"

"Your diagnostic information around lung growths."

"Your people suffer from such things? You appear in such good health."

Cassidy thought for a moment. "It's not that it's a common occurrence, but it is often difficult to diagnose early."

"And our testing could help?"

Cassidy started to nod, but caught herself. "Yes, I think it could."

Dr. Arasellie shrugged once. "And what are you offering in return?"

"That's what I wanted to ask you about. Is there some further test you could run on me? Anything that might give you something to help the children in particular?"

Dr. Arasellie pulled a strand of green hair that had fallen out of the low ponytail the rest of her hair was tied back into.

"The thing is, the only thing that could really help our children is more vitamin D."

"Is there any source other than the chuga?"

"Unfortunately, no," Dr. Arasellie said. "The increase in our birth rate has been both a blessing and a curse. I fear many children will not make it to adulthood."

Cassidy looked at the digital image of the child's lungs and thought back to her brief interaction with Trica the night before.

"I wish there was something I could do to help," Cassidy said.

"Do you really mean that?"

It was Elona who spoke.

"Yes, of course."

"Then come with me."

After leaving the lab, Elona took her in a brand new direction. They went back through the garden where she'd originally met Captain Kruz, but instead of going to the courtyard, she took her in the lift up to a quiet floor with only one door. There was a screen next to it, similar to the one next to the door in Cassidy's room.

The screen was a shifting series of colours. Elona touched squares creating a rainbow pattern. Then the door slid open.

"Come," Elona said, walking inside.

Cassidy followed, expecting to enter an office. What

she walked into instead was something akin to a war room.

In the centre was a large hexagonal table with a glass top. It was emitting an orange glow. No one was near it, but there were many soldiers at stations all around the room. Cassidy recognized one of them.

Lugo got up from a monitor and approached them, a frown on his face.

"Why have you brought her here?"

"I don't answer to you," Elona said. "Where's the captain?"

Lugo's frown deepened. "I don't think he'll be happy—"

"What's happening here?" Captain Kruz came around a bank of monitors. He looked at Cassidy, but it was Elona he addressed. "Officer, explain."

"Of course, Captain. Could we go to your office?"

Captain Kruz didn't answer, but he turned on his heel and walked back around the bank of monitors. Elona and Cassidy followed, along with Lugo. Cassidy wasn't sure what they were going to talk about, but she would have preferred the young man stayed back. She wasn't alone in her feelings, at least not if Elona's tight lips were anything to go by.

Captain Kruz's office was a glass fronted room that looked out on more computer stations. There were a few officers working, but none looked up at their presence. Cassidy assumed their training was overriding their curiosity.

The office was sparse, just a table with a monitor and no place to sit, not even for the Captain.

"Now then, what's this about?" The Captain looked to Elona.

"While in conversation with Dr. Arasellie, Cassidy suggested she could make a trade. That perhaps there was something she could do to help us and in return there was medical information we have that would be helpful to her people."

Captain Kruz's frowned, puzzled. "What could we possibly have that could be helpful to such a healthy people?"

Cassidy described the test for lung cancer. "But Dr. Arasellie made it clear that running further tests on me would not be useful."

"No, tests wouldn't help, but there's something else you could do for us," Elona said, looking back to the captain. "Isn't there?"

The Captain looked Cassidy over as though seeing her for the first time.

"Yes, I think I understand what you are saying, Officer. I'll need to consult with the capital."

"Consult about what?" Cassidy asked.

But the captain didn't answer her question. "Return to your rooms, I'll be in touch soon."

Cassidy paced the small space in her room, counting her steps.

She had just passed the two thousand mark.

Captain Kruz had sent her back four hours earlier. Cassidy had asked if she could look around the domes instead, but Elona had explained there was no one to accompany her as all the officers had duties to attend to.

Cassidy didn't need an escort, but she wasn't surprised that the Alluvians weren't keen on letting an alien guest wander about all alone.

After the first hour, someone had come by with lunch.

By the second hour, Cassidy had gone through her backpack and cursed herself for not throwing in so much as a deck of cards.

Some vacation this was turning out to be.

She tried to figure out what it was that the Alluvians thought she could help with. Dr. Arasellie had been clear that no medical tests could help. All she really had going for her was her ability to breathe outside the dome and she wasn't sure how that could help anyone.

2,305 steps, 2,306, 2,307…

Supposing there was something she could do to help, would she?

It wasn't even a question really. Not only did she want to help the Alluvians, if the trade-off was technology that could reduce human suffering from cancer, of course she'd do whatever she could.

Assuming it was ethical.

When the panel on her door lit up, she tried not to get too hopeful. It was nearly suppertime, so it was just as likely to be an officer with a tray.

But when the door slid open, she saw it was Elona.

"The captain is ready to see you now."

# CHAPTER EIGHT

Cassidy stood next to Elona along one edge of the hexagonal table in the war room. If a six-sided table could have a head, Captain Cruz was standing at it. They were also joined by Lugo and a few other officers, some of whom Cassidy had met at supper the night before.

Professor Malen was also there, his posture still stiff, though he gave Cassidy a shrug of recognition.

Had it really only been just the one night since she'd arrived on Alluvia?

The stations around the room — the ones where hours before she'd seen officers seated in front of monitors — were now empty. Only those around the table were in attendance.

The captain had been the last to arrive and hadn't spoken yet. Instead, he was pushing buttons on the underside of the table. The glass top turned from a glowing topaz to a pale blue. Then everything shifted. It was as though things began to grow out of the table's surface. It took Cassidy only a moment to realize it was a model landscape.

"Is that a hologram?" She asked, reaching out to touch

a mountain. Her fingers went right through the peak.

"I don't know that word," Elona said. "It's an image made of light."

"This is Telluria," Captain Kruz said. "This model is based on our most up-to-date images that our processors have brought back."

"It's extraordinary technology," Cassidy said.

"You're not here to look at projections," Lugo said. "You're here to help."

Cassidy frowned but Captain Kruz cut Lugo a scathing look.

"You will be polite to our visitor."

"Our unexpected visitor," Lugo said, muttering under his breath. Evidently Captain Kruz didn't hear him because he continued speaking. He pointed to a grouping of large, cylindrical buildings.

"These silos are where the Tellerians keep their food supply."

"If this is to scale, those are enormous," Cassidy said.

"Yes, they have a good food supply on hand," Captain Kruz said. "Grown thanks to our fertilizer on these fields."

The captain used a metal pointer to pick out four fields, all near some kind of base. "These fields grow all the food for both Alluvia and Telluria, but only this field can grow the chuga."

"And that's a problem?" Cassidy asked.

"It is," the captain answered. "If we could grow chuga in two fields, we could produce enough to ensure our current generation reaches adulthood."

"Have you asked the Tellurians for their help?"

Lugo snorted. "Of course we asked for help. They refuse."

"And it's not like we can go there to set up the field ourselves," Elona said. "We can't leave our planet. That's where you come in."

Cassidy looked to the captain. "What exactly do you want from me?"

Captain Cruz pointed at the smallest field. "If we could convert this field here, that would be enough."

"What's involved in converting a field?"

"It's fairly simple, actually," Professor Malen spoke up. "There's an irrigation system running through each field, it's what's used to feed the fertilizer to the plants. All that's needed is to pour a treatment into the system and the plants in that field will produce higher amounts of vitamin D."

While the professor spoke, Captain Kruz magnified the image so that the smallest field dominated the table space.

"The irrigation system is housed just along here," the professor continued, pointing to a small triangular building. "Once you go inside, all you will need to do is pour the treatment into one of the vats and make sure it starts pumping out. The solution will turn a bright pink, that's how you will know it's working."

"That's it?" Cassidy looked from the professor to the captain. "That's all that's needed?"

"Given we can't go there ourselves," Professor Malen said, "it's basically an impossible task."

"Can't you send your robots?"

"No," Captain Kruz cut in. "The Tellurians don't have

much in the way of their own technology, but they do have an extensive alert system. Our robots cannot leave the landing base."

"So, you need me to go to the field on Telluria and feed the special concoction into the irrigation system?"

"Yes," Captain Kruz agreed. "And in exchange we will give you the information you were interested in, about the lung tests from Dr. Arasellie."

Cassidy leaned forward, taking a closer look at the hologram. This task was everything she loved. A space adventure, an undercover operation, a payoff that would help both Alluvians and humans.

"What reason did the Tellurians give for not treating the fields?"

Captain Kruz glanced at Professor Malen before speaking.

"Our races have been at odds for so long, there is little desire on their part to help us, particularly as there is nothing in it for the Tellurians. They do not need a vitamin D rich diet to survive."

"Perhaps if they knew how fragile our children are, they would change their minds," Professor Malen added. "However, we cannot risk bringing them to our planet and allowing them to see just how vulnerable we are to attack."

Cassidy tapped her chin in thought. It was a fair enough explanation. Certainly, humans were no less guilty of ignoring each other's suffering, especially when they couldn't see it for themselves.

The Tellurians were obviously the race with the most power here. They controlled the land, and they controlled the food supply — as evidenced by their silos. If not for their need for the fertilizer, it was likely they'd never make any accommodations for the Alluvians at all.

"How long before this mission takes place?"

Cassidy hadn't really thought about how long she would be staying, but her supposed trip to Cancun would come to an end eventually and she'd be expected to check in at home.

"We have a shipment going out tomorrow," Professor Malen said. "You could easily be accommodated."

That meant she could be heading home by this time on the following day with the answer to diagnosing early lung cancer in her back pocket. At that rate, she'd have time to go through the portal again before returning from her "vacation."

"All right," Cassidy said. "I'll do it."

# CHAPTER NINE

"Are you certain these clothes are all I will need to pass as a Tellurian?" Cassidy looked down at the flowing shirt and knee length breeches that Elona had delivered. Unlike the Alluvian items, these were in plain browns and taupes.

"Your colouring is not common, but it is not so unique that you will stand out," Elona said. "You will find that the Tellerians are much more pigmented than we are."

Cassidy picked up the clothes and settled them on the chair under the bed shelf. Since she had such an early rise in the morning, it was decided that as much as possible would be prepared the night before.

"You will be leaving after your mission is over?" Elona asked. The officer had been present when Cassidy had told the captain of her plan.

"I think it's time to return. My family will be wondering where I am."

"I have enjoyed the experience of meeting you," Elona said with a small smile. "And I know if you are successful, we will all think of you often as we watch our children grow."

Cassidy swallowed hard. Elona had caught her off guard. Not that she was ever the most comfortable with others expressing feelings of gratitude toward her.

"I have enjoyed meeting you too. And I appreciate that you took the time to show me around your base."

Elona shrugged once. "I will leave you to rest."

When she was alone, Cassidy crawled into bed wearing the Alluvian version of pyjamas — not that different from the clothing she'd worn to supper. They were comfortable and she wondered if she could fit them into her backpack to take home.

Much like the night before, the bed shelf was comfortable, and she drifted off while watching the light outside her window slowly dim.

The next morning Cassidy awoke to the glow of the Alluvian equivalent of dawn just as the panel next to her door lit up.

A young officer entered with a breakfast tray and told her she should start getting ready.

Cassidy was still adjusting to Alluvian time measurement, but she figured she had about half an hour before the officer returned. Not that it would take her long to prep.

After breakfast, she got a dry shower and changed into the comfortable Tellurian clothes. She'd just finished braiding her hair when the panel lit up again and the same young officer was there to show her to the hangar bay.

The officer never introduced himself and seemed jumpier than Elona. At a guess, Cassidy figured he was of a junior rank. As they walked through the corridors, he had a hard time hiding his curious looks in her direction.

Cassidy was relieved when they arrived at the hangar and the young officer was dismissed, though based on the look on his face, she wasn't the only one.

Evidently not all Alluvians were comfortable meeting aliens.

The dome housing the hangar was the biggest space Cassidy had yet entered by far. At its centre was a black ship whose shape she could best equate to a sleek bus. There were two other ships off to the side, which she assumed were used as back-up.

A stream of scientists wheeled heavy crates up to the open doors at the front of the ship where a shiny black robot picked them up as though they were filled with feathers and stacked them onto the ship.

There was a group of officers to one side and Cassidy was less than excited to see that the only one she recognized was Lugo. He broke off from the others to join her.

"You look Tellurian," he said, looking her up and up down.

"Thanks," Cassidy said, with a smirk. "That's the point."

She wasn't sure if Lugo ignored her sarcasm because it went over his head or, more likely, because he still didn't like her. If it were the latter, the feeling was mutual.

"You'll have a limited window of time to move about the planet," Lugo said. "Once the robots finish unloading and then reloading, the ship will need to return whether you are on board or not."

Cassidy nodded. "The field is nearby. I won't need long."

"You will have to ensure no one sees you getting off

or on the ship," Lugo said, stepping to one side so that Cassidy could see a large empty crate. "The bots have been programmed to take this particular crate to a covered area on the landing field. You should be able to get out undetected. The bots are also programmed to pack this crate up last."

"So I'll need to be back inside when the bot returns for me? Sounds easy enough."

"Glad you think so."

Cassidy saw Professor Malen and Captain Kruz approach and was grateful it wasn't just her and Lugo any longer.

Professor Malen had two air tanks, each one about the size of a two-litre soda bottle, and a helmet with a hose attached.

It was similar to the get-up Cassidy had seen the scientist wearing at the lab the day before.

"This will be your air source to and from the planet."

Of course, there wasn't air circulating on the ship. That would be a waste with it just being the bots.

"There are extra air tanks on board the ship that I'll show you before take off," Professor Malen continued. "Along with the canister you'll need to feed into the irrigation system."

Cassidy strapped the canisters to her back but wouldn't put the helmet on until take off.

"I'd also like you to wear this," Captain Kruz handed her what looked like a round black brooch covered in colourful geometric patterns. "There's a button on the back that you should use if there's any sign of trouble from the Tellurians."

"Will it alert you back here?"

"Yes."

"Got it," Cassidy said, pinning it to her collar.

As she boarded the ship for the journey, Cassidy saw that Elona and Dr. Arasellie were standing near the hangar bay doors. Both waved to her, though she couldn't help noticing that Elona looked unhappy.

Likely she was nervous, as Cassidy should be.

A seat with a belt had been installed on the ship, though as the door closed Cassidy wished it had occurred to someone to install a light or a window. She was not naturally claustrophobic, but having only glowing robot eyes for company was not her idea of a fun time.

Still, she was about to travel through space, and nothing beat that.

Professor Malen had explained how it would all work, so even though she couldn't see, she could still picture what was happening.

All the Alluvians would have cleared out of the hangar in anticipation of take off. Cassidy could feel the rumbling sensation as the engine started.

The dome they were in was specially constructed for the ceiling to open up, which would allow the ship access to the sky. Just over the engines, she could hear a scraping sound and pictured the roof above them opening like a roof on a convertible.

Though, she thought to herself, that was probably not an accurate representation.

The engine noise grew louder, and she assumed they were propelling upward, into the atmosphere. Her body stuck to the seat, gravity pushing her back as the ship climbed ever higher until the force lessened and she felt herself grow weightless. She was grateful for the seatbelt. While it would have been neat to float around, bumping into things in the dark did not feel like fun.

Fortunately, everything else on the ship had been secured somehow, even the robots.

Cassidy had tried to estimate the length of the voyage and her best guess was a few hours, though, since she couldn't move enough to get a flashlight to check her watch, there was no way for her to keep time anyway.

She took calming breaths and told herself she was lucky. How many humans got to experience the sensation of floating aimlessly in the darkness of space?

# CHAPTER TEN

They were landing.

At least, Cassidy was almost certain that's what they were doing.

At some point she'd entered a pseudo meditation, letting her mind wander in a sort of waking dream. She pictured her family, wondering what sorts of things they might be up to. Her dad was probably trying to find someone to beat at Scrabble. The thought brought a smile to her face.

The feel of the engines shifting as the ship encountered more friction brought her back to the present. Sure enough, her body grew heavier and heavier until she once again felt gravity weighing her down.

The ship jolted as it hit the ground and Cassidy remained in her seat until the sound of the engine became a dull whirring. She unbuckled her seatbelt and pulled a small flashlight out of her pocket. She had a short amount of time to get in the crate before the ship's doors would open and a Tellurian peeked in.

Cassidy's legs felt like jelly as she stood, and she very nearly fell forward on her face. Fortunately, she caught herself on the edge of a crate — as luck would have it, her crate. She stepped inside, still wearing the helmet and air tanks. It made her movements clumsy, but she needed an air source until she was off the ship. She pulled down the lid, hoping she wouldn't have to wait around for long.

The floor beneath the crate began to vibrate and was accompanied by the creaking of the ship's door opening. Cassidy braced herself. She knew her crate would be one of the first ones to be unloaded and the last to be reloaded.

The crate was jerked upward, and the canister Professor Malen had packed for her task rolled toward her. Cassidy caught it and stuffed it into the rough cloth messenger bag she'd been given for this exact purpose.

She felt the robot's stilted steps and listened as they transitioned from echoing off the ship's metal floor to the dull thunk of the ground.

The crate was lowered with a thud. Evidently the robots had not been programmed to account for living cargo. Cassidy waited a few extra moments while the sound of the robot moved off. She removed the helmet and air tanks, making sure the valves were off so that air didn't leak out. Then she opened the lid on the crate.

The first thing she did was take a deep breath.

It felt like the first time her lungs had really been full in days. She thought she'd grown accustomed to the thinner air in the domes but she grew lightheaded and her chest fluttered as she breathed in the earthy Tellurian air.

Still, it felt good.

After a few more breaths her heart rate slowed to a more moderate pace and she was able to take in her surroundings.

Cassidy's crate had been put down on a landing platform that was covered in square brown tiles that bounced under her feet. Between the tiles, tall, spiky leaves poked out. In front of her, at the edge of the platform was a veritable forest.

It had only been days since she'd left earth, but she'd missed vegetation, though the plant-life surrounding her right now was hardly anything she'd see on earth. The trees here were tall — easily the equivalent of two or three storeys — and were covered in deep green foliage.

Cassidy looked up; the sky was covered in clouds, but it wasn't cold. She wished the clouds would move off so she could see the color of the Tellurian sky, but the sound of robots moving about reminded her that she was on a timeline.

Her crate had been set up around the back of the ship. Being close to the forest meant that she hadn't been seen yet. She moved around the side of the ship and peeked out at the front where robots were unloading the crates of fertilizer. A group of Tellurians waited nearby, surrounding their own crates — presumably filled with food.

Just like in the images she'd seen in the gallery on her first night in Alluvia, the Tellurians had hair and skin in varying dark shades. It was as though all the colour had been sucked out of the planet below and now resided on the moon.

One Tellurian in particular — a male with rusty red skin — stood out from the others. Mostly because he literally stood away from the crowd, observing what was happening.

Recalling the hologram map, Cassidy knew she needed to step away from the landing pad and take a right on the road in front of the ship. Since no one was looking in her direction, she left the cover of the ship, ducking around crates, until she was able to set foot off the landing pad and onto the road.

She joined a stream of Tellurians, hurrying in both directions. Many held baskets and Cassidy assumed it must be a market day — which would make her job easier. It was always better to have a crowd to blend into.

As she headed in the direction of the field, she had the sensation like someone was watching her, but a quick glance around showed nothing amiss. Her clothes and hair blended in easily enough.

The further she got from the landing pad, the more the crowd dispersed until she was alone on the road, the tall skinny trees rising up on either side of her. In the distance she could make out the massive silos housing the Tellurian food supply, which meant the field was close by.

She rounded a bend and there it was, spread out before her. A field of bluish crops. They weren't as blue as the chuga she'd eaten on Alluvia, but they were still alien enough.

Cassidy only gave herself a few moments to take in the foreign landscape before finding the small, triangular building that housed the irrigation system. It sat on a back corner of the field, with forest just behind.

All around the field were wooden posts with glass spheres at the top. Cassidy assumed those were the sensors that would detect robots. She edged her way around the field, hoping the door to the building wasn't under some kind of intense security system. That was the one thing the Alluvians hadn't been able to account for. Cassidy had a few lock-picking tools in her messenger bag, but nothing that could get around a really advanced system.

When she got closer, she saw that the building was made of wood and wasn't as large as it had appeared from a distance. She also noticed that it had no security system to speak of, though there was another wooden pole next to the entrance with a glass sphere on top.

The door handle was a lever — a large one, about the length of her forearm. Cassidy cranked it to one side and was surprised to find that the door swung open.

*They're very trusting of each other*, she thought to herself and then felt a twinge of guilt. She was breaching that trust.

Though, she reminded herself she wasn't performing sabotage. It wasn't like she was about to ruin the fields. She was making it so that they could grow better plants. Plants that could help the Alluvian children.

An overhead light came on as the door opened, and Cassidy saw that the set-up inside was fairly simple — exactly as Professor Malen had explained. The room had three walls, one of which had four glass vats lined up side by side with their spouts attached to pipes ran into the floor and presumably out into the fields.

The solution in the vats was clear. It might have been ordinary water. There were openings at the top, but the vats were just tall enough to be out of Cassidy's reach. She looked around but there was no furniture.

With nothing to stand on and the vats too slippery to climb, Cassidy knew she had to think fast. One of the vats was close to a corner and the walls were a rough wood. Cassidy was grateful she'd decided to accessorize the Tellurian clothing with her own boots.

Setting up in the corner, she managed to get one foot, then the other, off the floor and balanced on the walls. It was just enough height to reach the top.

Opening the lid, she took out the canister Professor Malen had given her and poured the contents in. She lost her balance just as the canister emptied.

Hitting the floor, she kept her eyes on the vat.

For a few excruciating seconds nothing happened.

Then the water inside turned pink.

She'd done it!

There was a deafening screech.

An alarm.

Now she really had done it.

# CHAPTER ELEVEN

The door crashed back against the wall as Cassidy pushed it open in her haste to get away from the field.

Standing on the doorstep to the irrigation building, she could see that the glass sphere on the post outside the door was lit up a bright blue. In fact, all the spheres out in the field were lit up.

"Oh no," Cassidy muttered. This wasn't good.

In the distance, from the direction of the silos, she could see a group Tellurians heading toward her. Under other circumstances, she would have appreciated the rainbow of colors made by the varying shades of their skin and hair. However, all it did at the moment was highlight how large their group was.

If she hurried, Cassidy figured she could run in the direction of the landing pad and blend in with the market crowds before breaking off and jumping back into the crate.

Nothing to it.

Except, there was another group of Tellurians coming from that direction.

And, of course, the alarms were still blaring incessantly.

She ducked back behind the irrigation building, hoping she hadn't been seen. What she needed was a plan.

"What you need is a distraction."

For the briefest moment, Cassidy couldn't process that the voice she heard hadn't come from her own head. Then she saw a reddish skinned male duck out from the trees. She recognized him immediately as the male she'd seen earlier, when she'd first come out of the crate — the one who'd been standing away from the rest of the group.

"Were you following me?" Cassidy called over the noise. Up close she could see that his eyes were an intense shade of yellow.

"Luckily, yes. Now hand me that pendant you're wearing."

Cassidy's hand closed over the broach as the stranger's eyes settled on it. She'd just been evaluating her situation and trying to decide whether or not she should use it.

"I can't do that."

"We need a distraction and that is certain to get us one."

Even over the alarms, Cassidy could hear the sound of angry mob voices.

"This is just a communicator," she said, though she wasn't certain if that was the case. It hadn't been made clear. It could be a tracker. "What can it do?"

The stranger snorted. "That's not a communicator. It's a personal detonator. If you press the button on the back, there'll be an explosion."

Cassidy's heart stuttered in her chest. "No, that's not possible."

The stranger didn't offer further explanation. He reached through her fingers and pulled at the broach, tearing the fabric on her tunic in the process.

"Cover your ears," he said, pressing down on the button on the back of the pendant — the one she'd been instructed to press when she completed her mission— and hurling it away from them. The explosion went off in midair, near the tops of the trees.

Cassidy had clapped her hands over her ears just in time. The ground shook beneath their feet, but both she and her companion had braced themselves in time to avoid tumbling over.

"That detonated," Cassidy said, shaking her head as she looked in the direction the bomb had gone off.

If she'd pressed that button, she would have been killed.

"We need to get you back to the ship."

The stranger grabbed her arm, pulling her toward the woods. As he ran down a trail, Cassidy stayed close on his heels. She had no time to ask who he was, or why he'd decided to help her.

"This is a shortcut. Your ship is just up ahead."

Part of Cassidy wasn't sure she even wanted to return to the planet. She'd trusted the Alluvians and they'd nearly blown her up.

Not to mention the stranger she was following. What was his story?

But the portal was on that planet. She needed to return if she was going to make it home again. And she was going to get that information about lung testing — the Alluvians most definitely owed her.

The trees grew closely together, filtering out what light there was from the overcast sky and making it feel much later. Cassidy couldn't make out any path to speak of, but somehow her companion was able to move with confidence.

For all she knew, he could have been leading her anywhere. Still, he could have let her blow herself up, so weighing all possibilities, he seemed worth trusting.

They didn't have to run for too long and soon enough Cassidy could see the trees thinning. The stranger came to a stop.

"Your ship is just through there."

Cassidy could make out the back of the landing pad through the trees. She moved closer to the edge of the woods for a better look and her stomach dropped. Whereas there had been stacks of crates when she'd left, the area was almost completely cleared out — except for her crate.

She was out of time.

"I need to go," Cassidy said, looking at the stranger and attempting to memorize the details of his appearance — particularly the intelligent yellow eyes. She wanted to be able to recall the face of the person who'd helped her. "But thanks for your help."

"I'm sure we'll meet again," the stranger said with a half-smile.

Cassidy wanted to explain that that wasn't possible — that she wouldn't be able to return. That this was well and truly it.

But at that moment, one of the robots began rounding its way toward the crate. She needed to move, fast.

"Good-bye!" She called, tearing her way out of the woods.

She ran for all she was worth toward the crate, the springy tiles giving her a bit of extra momentum. There was no opportunity for stealth, no way to confirm no one was watching. She kept her eyes forward, watching as the robot got ever closer to its target.

Had they always moved that fast? Surely not.

With an extra push of adrenalin, she put her head down and bolted toward the crate.

# CHAPTER TWELVE

The trip back wasn't as fun.

Instead of a pleasant, meditative doze, Cassidy's mind raced over what had happened on the moon.

She'd trusted the Alluvians. She'd agreed to this mission to help their children. Yet, had they trusted her? If she'd gotten into trouble, they would have allowed her to blow herself up. Were they even intending for her to come back?

More importantly, were they intending to let her leave?

She knew she'd need to be on her guard when she returned. She also knew that her trip was at an end. It was definitely past time to leave Alluvia.

When the ship landed, Cassidy stayed put in her seat and took a few calming breaths. The air in the tank had been an adjustment after breathing the Tellurian air. All the more reason to head home.

Cassidy unbuckled her seatbelt and took off the helmet and tanks. She followed one of the robots down the ramp and off the ship. With the robot in front of her, she was able to see the Alluvians before they saw her. Captain Kruz and Professor Malen were holding an animated conversation, broad smiles on their faces. Those smiles dropped for a fraction of a second when the robot moved, and they saw Cassidy.

It was all the confirmation she needed. They hadn't expected her to return.

The captain recovered first. He walked toward her, smile firmly back in place.

"Cassidy! Our hero."

She forced a smile in return. "Happy to help."

Captain Kruz's gaze landed on the tear in her tunic where the stranger had torn her broach off, and his eyes narrowed.

"You didn't encounter any problems?"

"No, nothing of note. Though I did lose the broach you gave me. But you were still able to see that the mission was a success?"

"Yes, we had satellite images."

Likely they'd seen the explosion then.

"How fortunate," Cassidy said. Her face was starting to feel tight from smiling.

"You must let us throw a dinner in your honor," Captain Kruz continued. "It's the least we can do."

"I appreciate the offer, but I must return to my ship. It has been a few days now and I wouldn't want any of my colleagues to feel like they should come looking for me."

"Of course," Captain Kruz said, his smile faltering again. "We wouldn't want that."

"If I could just see Dr. Arasellie, I'll be on my way."

"Dr. Arasellie?"

"Yes. For the exchange."

Captain Kruz took a step back. "I'm sure she'll be more than happy to see you."

Dr. Arasellie was not happy, exactly, more curious. Cassidy had insisted on going to her room to change back into her own clothes before heading to the lab. She stood by the window, watching the vecas, while the doctor prepped her information.

"Here you go," Dr. Arasellie handed her a printout. Cassidy looked it over to confirm it was the information she needed, then rolled it into a scroll and zipped it into an inside pocket on her jacket.

"Thanks," Cassidy said, turning away from the window. She was about to head to the door when Dr. Arasellie's words stopped her.

"You really have saved our children."

She nodded, but didn't trust herself to respond. What could she say? She hoped the Alluvian youth grew up to be better behaved than the current crop of adults?

Elona was waiting for her outside the lab. She couldn't look Cassidy in the eye which confirmed her suspicion that Elona also hadn't expected her to return.

"I'm to escort you back out of the complex," she said.

"Lead the way," Cassidy said.

It appeared the lie she'd told Captain Kruz upon her return had worked. Without the threat of retaliation from more "unexpected visitors" she likely would never have made it off the complex alive.

They passed back through the courtyard where she'd seen officers during her first visit, but it was empty now. She wasn't sure if that was because it wasn't a mealtime, or because they were told to steer clear until she left.

When they arrived at the corridor where she'd originally entered the compound, Elona stopped at the panel next to a door. When she spoke, her words came out in a rush.

"I'm glad you made it back."

Elona didn't wait for a response. She pushed a code into the panel — causing it to change from blue to yellow — and stood back as the door opened to reveal the black vehicle she'd arrived in.

"Did you want a ride to your ship?" Elona asked, though she didn't appear surprised when Cassidy said no.

"I'll leave you here then."

"Thanks for everything." Cassidy waved as the door between them closed. All things considered, it was a friendly goodbye. Holding a grudge felt pointless when they weren't likely to see each other again and Elona had looked contrite.

Perhaps she'd learned a lesson.

A few seconds after the door to the corridor closed, the doors in front of the vehicle opened and Cassidy stepped outside. She'd already put her scarf around her neck in anticipation of the air, but the stench still hit full force. It felt like it coated her nostrils and tongue.

Cassidy set out, glancing around as she left. She'd been in a windowless vehicle upon arrival so hadn't gotten the opportunity to see the domes up close from the outside.

The entrance she left through was wide — it had to be to accommodate the vehicles. And the metal poles she'd seen upon arrival were spaced a few meters apart, creating a path to that door.

Further down she could see another entrance. It was smaller and there was no sign of surveillance poles. If she were ever to come back, that's the direction she would go in.

Though, she was most definitely never coming back.

# CHAPTER THIRTEEN

The cave entrance could not have appeared soon enough.

Sure, she'd adjusted to the smell. At least, as much as a person could adjust to such a foul presence. But the trek had felt longer this time, not only because she'd been driven part of the way on her trip there, but also because she'd already had a very full day.

Just that morning she'd gotten up and gone to a moon.

Now it was dark. She'd watched the brownish sun fade over the horizon of the dying planet in what was certain to be one of the saddest sunsets ever witnessed. She'd taken out her flashlight, since she'd discovered the Tellurian moon provided no moonlight, and had finally made her way back to the cave.

Inside the tunnel she took a moment to appreciate how the beam of her flashlight reflected off the shiny rock while she ate a granola bar from her stash. She hadn't wanted to risk even a snack from the Alluvians before leaving.

She couldn't wait to get back to earth. She was going to eat the biggest basket of fries.

She followed the tunnel, grateful that she hadn't had to memorize any twists or turns. She finished her bar and stowed the wrapper in her bag as she came upon the portal cave. Again, she was taken in by how shiny the surfaces around her were and for a moment, she wasn't sure where the portal was, but she held out her hand and felt a cool shock to her fingers.

That was different. On the way in she'd felt warm.

She pushed her fingers forward and the cave wall gave way. Definitely the portal.

Adjusting her pack and sticking her flashlight into a jacket pocket, she stepped through and saw a flash of light, like a crack in the cave wall to her right. She remembered seeing something similar on her arrival.

There was no time for reflection as she was immediately gripped by a cold sensation.

Odd.

Then there was the light. Even with her eyes closed it was blinding. Not soft and blue like when she'd arrived. This light was stark white.

She stumbled through, her arm covering her eyes as she emerged in the cave back on earth. She pulled her arm away and blinked rapidly. She couldn't see anything, but of course it was dark in the cave.

Cassidy felt around in her pocket and found her flashlight. She turned it on, but she still couldn't make out more than shadows. That portal had really done a number on her eyes.

She managed to make her way out of the cave, into a moonless night. She kept her flashlight, trying to maneuver to the road where her car was. Hopefully her vision cleared soon so she could drive herself home. She didn't really want to spend the night in her car.

The beam of her light flickered off rocks and mud and Cassidy thought her vision was coming around. She could make out the shape and color of the tall spiky plants.

Wait.

She came to a stop and ran her light over the plant again.

That wasn't earth vegetation.

"Freeze!" A loud voice called from her right and, all of a sudden, the area was flooded with light and she could see that she wasn't on earth after all. The voice continued speaking and Cassidy heard the sound of footsteps surrounding her on all sides.

"You are hereby under arrest for crimes against Telluria."

# THE TELLURIAN TERRORIST

LAURALANA DUNNE & JD RYOT

# CHAPTER ONE

Cassidy stood tall in the cold, expansive hall. Head back and feet shoulder-width apart, she kept her spine straight as the tribunal filed back into the room.

It had been two days since the Tellurians had apprehended her. Two days since she had fallen through the wrong portal from Alluvia and ended up on the moon.

Cassidy grimaced. It was the first time she had ever encountered that particular phenomenon—multiple gateways in one location—and it hadn't helped that the rock system was identical between the three planets. She hadn't even known she wasn't on Earth until the Tellurian guards had picked her up walking down the dusty road. She realized something was amiss when they stopped their vehicle and got out to stare at her.

Humans and Tellurians didn't exactly share the same coloring. And while Cassidy's appearance seemed to be smack-dab in the middle of the two peoples—her hair too pale to be Tellurian, but her skin too vibrant to be Alluvian—her copper-colored hair was a dead giveaway.

The sound of a throat being cleared interrupted her thoughts and she snapped her gaze to the front of the room. She winced when she realized that this was not the first attempt to get her attention.

Five scowling faces were turned toward her.

"If you are ready, Ms. Cane?" the Tribunal Magistrate, an elderly woman with deep lilac-coloured skin and pale orange eyes, asked in a tone laced with irritation.

Cassidy ducked her head, feeling sheepish, and attempted to look remorseful. "Of course, Ma'am. I apologize."

The man sitting to the right of the woman sniffed critically. "Head Magistrate," he corrected, his salmon-coloured eyes hard.

This was not going well. Cassidy winced. "Apologies, Head Magistrate. I meant no disrespect." She reverently hoped that the Magistrates couldn't change their ruling mid-announcement. By the expressions on their faces, any favours that she may have won while presenting her defense had certainly disappeared.

"Ms. Cane," the Head Magistrate began, straightening in the centre chair. "You have been brought before us today on three different charges. We have heard your statement in response to your arrest. The two lesser charges are trespassing and theft. How do you plead?"

Cassidy cleared her throat. "Not guilty," she responded, feeling a twinge of accomplishment when her voice didn't waver.

One of the magistrates snorted and the Head Magistrate shot him a look. He stiffened with a scowl. She turned back to Cassidy. "Based on the ludicrous answers that you provided to our questions, this court has not only found you guilty of both charges, but we have also added the charge of contempt for making such a mockery of these proceedings. As for the higher charge: treason—"

"Wait, what?" Cassidy stepped forward. There had been no mention of treason at any point during the questioning. She knew nothing of the Tellurian's legal system—she had been operating blindly while trying to appeal to their sense of justice—but she had never heard of a situation where a treason charge was a good thing.

"We find you guilty," the Head Magistrate continued, as if Cassidy had never interrupted. The elderly woman stood and drew herself up to her full height. The other magistrates followed suit. A single shaft of light flickered to life and illuminated the area in front of her. "We will reconvene tomorrow after the median hour for sentencing."

The woman held her hands under the beam of light and clapped. The reverberations spread to the ends of the room, and Cassidy felt her bones rattle with the finality of the gesture. The beam switched off as the magistrates turned and shuffled from the room without so much as a backward glance toward her. Five heads of dark hair disappeared behind the closing door.

"Wait!" Cassidy called again. Rough hands grabbed her upper arms before she could take another step, and Cassidy was hauled backward. She struggled against the strong grip that held her, but it was to no avail. She was being pulled into the hallway.

Digging her heels into the door frame, she flexed her legs and was rewarded when the guard that held her grunted in surprise.

"There's been a mistake," Cassidy twisted her torso

to look up at his impassive face, but he just rolled his eyes and gave her petite form another tug. "I have to speak to them!"

With a snort, he dislodged her boots from the frame and dragged her from the room. The lightweight door zipped closed behind them with an upbeat chime, and Cassidy felt as though her only chance to reason her way out of this was cut off by the perky automated door.

# CHAPTER TWO

Cassidy rubbed her hands together with more force than was necessary. Originally, when she had been returned to her holding cell, her heart had been pounding. That familiar excited feeling that she enjoyed — the tingling in her fingertips — had given her a high as she bounced around the small room, looking for a way to secure her escape. Hours later, alone and in the dark, she had finally given up her search.

She rubbed her hands together again to release her frustration before plopping down on the thin metal wall shelf that served as her cot.

The holding cell was unlike any that she had seen before, or been in… not that she had availed of many in the past. It was a singular room, but a force shield kept her confined to the back half of it — much like a specimen in a glass cage. Observers were free to enter the room from the large doorway that connected it to the hallway.

Observers, or interrogators.

Cassidy felt her stomach drop. She had spent several unsuccessful hours fiddling with the shield trying to figure out a way to stall its activation. Whenever she came too close to the metal lip on the floor, its sensor would pick up on her proximity and activate. There was nothing to do now but wait.

With a huff, she lay back on the cot. Morning would arrive soon. She would have to figure out a plan before her sentencing, otherwise her only option would be to try to escape during the transfer, and without knowing her way around that would be inconvenient at best.

Closing her eyes, Cassidy ran over everything she had learned in her short time on the moon. Maybe she would find some new information while sifting through her memories.

A soft click caught her attention. Cassidy held her breath as a harsh beam of light swept the holding cell, illuminating the backs of her eyelids as it passed over her. There was another soft click, and the room was plunged into darkness once more as the door swung shut.

The light had come from the hallway. Someone was in her room.

Forcing herself to breathe softly despite the pounding of her heart, Cassidy strained her ears for the slightest hint of a sound. The hum of the force shield generator was the only constant in the room, but she was positive that she could hear careful footsteps drawing closer to her cell.

Cassidy gave a soft murmur and stretched, rolling onto her side so that her back was against the wall. Her arm dangled over the edge of the cot so that her fingertips grazed against the cold smoothness of the floor. She cracked her eyes open into slits, hoping for all the world that whoever was in the room with her was under the assumption that she had only shifted in her sleep.

Her controlled breathing seemed too loud in her ears. Finally, after what felt like hours, the soft padding of quiet footsteps began again, and the slightest hint of a moving shadow came into view.

With painstaking slowness, Cassidy extended her hand until she felt the cool rim of her meal tray. The food remained, uneaten, where she had tucked it out of the way under her cot. At the top of the tray, however, was the battered metal fork that had come with it.

Cassidy stretched her fingers and secured the handle. It was a pathetic excuse for a weapon, but she would make it work if she had to.

A low chuckle gave her pause. "I wouldn't bother with that if I were you," the voice murmured. "Even with the force shield turned off, the sensors are programmed to pick up on anything that might be considered a weapon. You'll set off the alarm."

The voice was strangely familiar. Cassidy remained motionless; the fork clutched firmly in her fist as she opened her eyes.

The figure continued toward her and stopped a few feet before reaching the force shield. "Why else do you think they'd risk giving it to you?"

The voice remained soft as it spoke. It wasn't for her benefit to try and keep her calm, Cassidy decided. It was soft because it was trying to avoid detection.

Keeping a firm grip on the flimsy utensil, Cassidy swung to her feet in a fluid motion. Realizing that the intruder didn't want to be discovered shifted some of the power in the room to her favour. Regardless of their intent, Cassidy had the ability to alert the outside guards if necessary. The room was obviously not soundproof if they were whispering.

Cassidy took a step toward the barrier between them. "Who are you?" She kept her voice even but refused to lower it, feeling a twinge of satisfaction when her hunch was rewarded by the figure's flinch.

His face came into view as he stepped closer. Wide, intense yellow eyes fastened themselves on her face as he inspected her, much as she did him. His hair was dark, as was the case with most Tellurians, but his skin held a rusty-red tinge that she found fascinating.

"A friend," he said simply.

"I doubt it," she snorted. "Breaking into my room in the middle of the night doesn't seem very friendly."

He smirked and took another step closer, and Cassidy was able to place him. He was the Tellurian on the landing platform who had helped her to escape after she'd been discovered converting the irrigation system to allow for extra Chuga growth. "Who said anything about breaking in? What if I'm looking to break you out?"

He was offering her help for the second time. His answer stemmed the questions that Cassidy wanted to barrage him with. Instead, she crossed her arms over her chest and cocked her head. "I'm listening."

*** 

He remained motionless. Waiting. Assessing her.

Cassidy did the same. The silence stretched between them as they stared at each other over the marker of the unactivated force shield.

He unclipped a disc from his belt and held it in the

palm of his hand. Cassidy watched as it stretched and ex-tended in a way that reminded her of a folding hand fan. Her guest stared at it for a brief moment before taking a step forward. She steeled her spine.

"How did you get to our moon?" His tone was care-fully neutral.

Cassidy realized it was a test. "The Alluvian cargo ship..."

He shook his head. "That was the first time. What about the second time? If you had your own ship, you wouldn't have returned here. You would have returned home."

Cassidy frowned. If he knew her story, then he had access to what she'd said in her defense hearing.

He sighed. "Your sentencing is tomorrow—"

"A portal," she blurted. She rubbed a palm against her thigh in agitation. Cassidy hated telling anyone about the portals. It was too big of a risk to let unknown alien races know how to get to Earth.

Technically she wasn't revealing any information about Earth. Just Alluvia, really. She calmed at the thought.

"I came here through a portal," she reiterated, squar-ing her shoulders. There was no help for it. She had to get out of here, now, and deal with this later. One problem at a time, she told herself.

He gave an unsurprised nod and took a step forward. "I want to hear all about it." He held her eye until she gave a nod, agreeing to his terms. Satisfied, he tossed the disc into the air between them. It sailed over the floor sensors and hovered there as the shield activated—a bright wall of light that shrank closer to the ground the lower that the disc fell.

The disc rested on the sensors, reflecting the shield back into its source so that there was a gap in the wall.

"Hurry," he urged.

He didn't have to tell her twice. Cassidy dropped her fork with a clatter and slipped through the gap, turning sideways in order to fit through the small opening that the device created.

Once both feet were firmly planted outside of the holding cell, Cassidy turned to inspect the disc that disrupted the field that she had tried so hard to disable.

She had little time to assess it before a high-pitched whine reached her ears. She stared, dumbfounded, as the thin metal disc crumpled under her gaze, folding in on itself and disappearing as though it had never existed in the first place.

She gave a low whistle. "That's one way to cover your tracks."

The man next to her gave another low chuckle. "That's at least one of the things I pride myself on being good at."

Cassidy raised a brow and he dipped into a quick bow. "My name is Aldan, Cassidy Cane. And I have been looking everywhere for you."

# CHAPTER THREE

Their escape from the government building went
much more smoothly than Cassidy had expected. Aldan
didn't use any technology to aid their flight. Instead, he
wove them on a timed, backtracking path along the corridors that somehow let them avoid all of the guards that
roamed the facility.

"There are others waiting for their hearings," he'd informed her as he eased open the door to her room, "so
security is increased. Our best bet is to stay undetected for
as long as possible so we can get out."

"And then?" Cassidy had asked, attempting to close
her door behind them as noiselessly as possible.

Aldan had given a wry smile. "Run."

As luck—or Alden's training—would have it, they
made it out without issue.

The chill of the outside hit Cassidy in the face as she
sprinted down the manicured path after the Tellurian. She
gulped down the night air, enjoying how fresh it felt in
comparison to the recycled, temperature-controlled stuff
she had been breathing for the past few days.

Aldan stopped without warning, and it was all she

could do to avoid colliding with him. He pivoted and grabbed her arm, giving it a tug as he dove behind the ornamental hedge lining the path. Cassidy followed after him.

They lay on their stomachs, panting, and attempted to catch their breaths. She turned to ask what they were doing, but Aldan raised a finger to his lips before she had the chance to speak.

She heard it then—the rumble of laughter accompanied by the sound of multiple footsteps. Several guards came up the hill, chatting among themselves as they made their way toward the building.

Shift change. Tellurians must have a heightened sense of hearing for Aldan to have picked up on their conversations from so far away.

Aldan raised himself up onto his elbows and watched them enter the building before letting out an exaggerated sigh. "That was close."

Cassidy cocked her head at him. "Was it? I feel like you've done this before a time or two."

"Once or twice," he grinned. Cassidy was struck by how the small expression lit up his face with mischief, making him appear youthful despite the gravity of the situation.

Cassidy couldn't help but grin in return. "Alright then. Since you're the expert: where to now?"

"Now? Now, we go. My craft is waiting."

Cassidy cast her eyes around, but all she could see was strange, flowering trees that dotted the rocky hills at random intervals. They reminded her of desert plants— large, spiked, weathered-looking things that jutted in all directions to fight for natural resources. They were nothing like the beautiful, delicate trees that grew in the Alluvian garden.

No grass grew anywhere in sight. The hedges and the trees were the only plant life next to them, and they only seemed to thrive due to the piles of the blue mulch heaped along their roots.

She raised her eyebrows in a question. There was no craft visible. The single point of entry into the complex was the stretching road that wove itself through a stone bridge and over a river that snaked through the property. There was no vehicle in sight.

"Craft?"

Aldan flopped onto the ground. "You didn't think we were going to walk, did you?" He winked and, before she could reply, stretched out and began to roll down the hill.

She watched, surprised, as he continued all the way to the bottom, stopping short of the rushing water and disappearing into the darkness of the shoreline's overgrowth — the only untended greenery around.

Cassidy waited for a telltale splash but heard nothing. Grumbling to herself, she followed suit and rolled into the darkness after him.

She came to a halt just before hitting the water. The thick, spiked plants that grew along the water's edge slowed her speed enough so that she could gain control of her descent.

Picking twigs out of her hair, Cassidy met the bemused gaze of Aldan. "Just a time or two?"

He grinned and gathered his feet beneath him. "Well,

maybe a time or four." He nodded ahead of them to the bridge. "We're almost there."

Cassidy rolled into a crouch and frowned. Not only was it the most unprotected spot in the whole complex, but it was also the most well-illuminated. Even the water plants around the bridge had been cut back to nothing.

"You want us to walk across the bridge," she asked in disbelief, careful to keep her voice low. "That's a terrible idea! The shift changeover is about to start."

Aldan waved his hand in dismissal. "Not walk. Fly."

When Cassidy blinked at him, he smirked. "Don't tell me that the Tellurian Terrorist is afraid of a little excitement."

Even in the dim lighting, Cassidy could see his pale eyes sparkle with the challenge, and she couldn't help but feel herself rise to it.

Her only response was a snort. Before he knew it, she launched herself forward and took off at a run, leaving him behind in her mad dash toward the bridge.

There was a muffled noise of surprise, and then the sound of even breathing as Aldan kept pace with her speed.

Cassidy resisted the urge to laugh. Despite herself, and the possible danger she was in, excitement was coursing through her veins and making her feel as though she were alive again.

A grumbling snagged her attention and Cassidy snapped her gaze to the quickly approaching road. A thick beam of light swept across the road as it rumbled toward the bridge.

"Get down!" Aldan hissed behind her.

Cassidy threw herself against the ground and was surprised to find that Aldan threw himself over her, covering her body with his own.

The light swept past them, and Cassidy jerked her head up in time to see a dilapidated vehicle, it's one lone headlight skimming across the road, sputter its way across the bridge and toward the building. She was able to distinguish the outlines of several passengers inside the vehicle.

If that's what stood for government technology on this planet, it was in worse shape than Cassidy had previously thought.

Several moments of tense silence passed. "You can get off of me now," she informed him, shifting her body to alleviate some of the weight on her pressure points.

"Sorry," he muttered. Instantly she felt lighter as shifted next to her. "My clothing blends into our surroundings better."

Cassidy couldn't fault him for that logic and dusted off her knees with a nod. "Now what?"

Aldan cocked his head and frowned. "You're right about the shift change. I can hear more vehicles on their way. More than usual. I wanted the distraction of the shift change to get you out, but I wasn't counting on the extra attention that tomorrow would bring."

"Extra attention?"

Aldan smirked. "It's not every day that you get to witness the sentencing of an off-worlder."

"Glad I could offer some distraction in these gloomy times," she quipped.

Aldan's smirk turned into a grin. He opened his mouth

to respond, but his expression faltered as more lights appeared in the distance.

Pulling up his sleeve, he tapped on a metal device around his wrist. A low-pitched whine filled the air around them. Cassidy took a step back when the surface of the river began to tremble.

She stood wide-eyed as water lapped furiously against the bank, cresting out in a convex shape by an unseen force above the river. The shape moved toward them from under the bridge.

Aldan tapped at his wrist again as there was a soft hiss. A porthole-sized opening rose outward, lifting mechanically out of thin air, and Cassidy could see the blinking lights of consoles floating in the space through it.

Aldan took one look at the approaching vehicles and stepped forward. He grabbed the rim of the opening and jumped through it. Cassidy was stunned to see him disappear, only to reappear a heartbeat later as he poked his head back through the opening. "Are you coming? The cover won't last for much longer!"

Cassidy gaped at him. He was sitting in a cloaked ship!

Her excitement was electrifying. Cassidy grabbed at the top of the opening and was shocked to find that she could grab the solid, cool material of the structure around it—even if she couldn't see it. Ignoring the lurch of her disconnected senses, she used both hands to lift herself up and swung herself through the opening after Alden...

—and landed right in a plush leather seat.

She tried not to let her jaw drop as her eyes roamed the inside of the craft. Blinking lights and controls were spread around her, taking up almost every space that the wall had to offer around the windows. Cassidy shook her head in disbelief. Everything inside the craft was invisible to the outside, but she had no trouble seeing the world around them.

"Buckle up," Aldan instructed, pressing a large button in the center console. The porthole cover hissed in response and began to close. He sat in the pilot's seat in front of her, settling into it as easily as she settled into her office chair at home. However, instead of grading student papers, he was tapping codes into the keypad in front of him to bring the machine around them to life.

The hatch clicked closed next to her, and Cassidy jumped as the locking mechanism's activation reverberated around them. She hastily buckled herself into her chair.

Mechanical lights stretched like glowing spider webs across the windows of the craft and Aldan swore under his breath.

"What's wrong?" Cassidy leaned forward and pressed her nose to the glass but could see nothing amiss outside around them.

"The cover is destabilizing."

"Meaning…?"

"Meaning we will be very visible, very shortly." He reached above himself and tapped finger on the glass over a gauge, as if telling it to hurry up. Cassidy watched the pointer tick up to the top level of the display with painstaking slowness. When it reached the top, an alert sounded, and Aldan breathed a sigh of relief.

"Finally," he muttered, settling back into his seat. His

fingers flew across the console, activating the engines and increasing their dull whine to a muted roar. "Cabin's pressurized. Hold on."

The craft jerked ahead with surprising speed. Cassidy clutched the flimsy arms of her chair as they shot down the river, the spray left in their wake slopping over the foliage and soaking the dusty shore.

Aldan pulled down on a large gear shift and the craft tipped back, the nose of the machine pointing up toward the lightening sky. The engines powered up and propelled them into the sky with a thunderous boom.

There was the sound of crumpling metal, and Cassidy watched as a piece of the craft detached and spiraled to the ground below. "Aldan…" Apparently all the machines on Telluria were in need of repair.

"It's fine. We got out of there just in time." He tapped the windshield, and Cassidy realized that the metallic glow had disappeared. "Our cover blew."

Cassidy peered out of the window. The craft's wings were visible, but there was no one around to see them. Clouds sped past them as they accelerated to dizzying heights. "Where are we going?"

Alden looked back at her and raised a brow. His coloring was more striking in the growing daylight—rusty red skin, dark hair, and daffodil-yellow eyes that mirrored the color of the clouds as they began to wake up for the day. Other than that, he looked like he could fit in at any cafe on earth. He looked positively human.

"We're going somewhere safe where we can talk. You promised to answer my questions, and once you do, I promise to take you home."

Cassidy tilted her head, noting that he had yet to level off their ascent. "And where, exactly, is that?"

Aldan tapped what looked to be coordinates into a map screen. When he caught her watching him, he rolled his eyes but didn't bother switching it off. They both knew she would never be able to recreate the journey.

"You'll see."

# CHAPTER FOUR

They had been flying for what felt like hours. At no point did Aldan turn the aircraft any great degree or reduce their height. Instead, it was almost like he had enacted some type of cruise control that kept their heading and speed constant—something that would have worried Cassidy had he not been so attentive in their surroundings.

"Do you think we're being followed?" She asked at one point, noting how his attention kept shifting from the radar screen to the cloud-obstructed view around them.

"As a result of your break-out? No. I doubt it."

Cassidy felt her pulse pick up at his response. "But resulting from something else…?"

Aldan inclined his head, his eyes trained on the airspace around them. "Possibly. It depends on what the others have been up to."

Cassidy sat up straight in her chair. "Others?" When his only response was a shrugged shoulder, she crossed her arms. "You're leaving out a lot of information."

"That's something we have in common."

Cassidy settled back into her chair and said nothing.

The wind shifted and a mountain peak loomed in the distance. The rocky tip speared through the cloud cover, looking before them like a desolate beacon as Aldan maneuvered the craft toward it.

He grabbed a headband and positioned the attached yellow lens over one eye. To her surprise, he flicked off the navigation switches around him, powering everything down except for the engines.

Cassidy could feel a low rumble throughout her body. "What is that?"

"The volcano." He nodded toward the mountain peak.

It became louder the closer they came, and Cassidy could feel the thrumming in her ribcage despite being buckled securely in a pressurized cabin.

"The magma constantly churns inside of the mountain, circulating the molten rock. Whatever the rock is made of jams our electronic signals—"

"—making it the perfect place to hide," Cassidy finished. When Alden nodded, she frowned. "But what if the volcano blows its top?"

"That's when things get extra exciting."

Cassidy felt a twinge of annoyance at his cavalier attitude. "And what constitutes 'regular exciting?'" She'd been stuck inside a cramped aircraft for almost an entire day, unable to do anything but stare out a window and shift her weight in her seat. She was pretty sure her backside had become numb as a result. So far, her sentencing hearing would have been more interesting.

Aldan tapped a code into the console with a smirk. "This."

The engine output decreased immediately. There was a brief stutter of motion, then the craft began to fall. Cassidy refused to scream as she felt her stomach lurch up into her throat. Instead, she dug her fingers into the back of his chair in a death grip, her knuckles turning white.

Aldan laughed at her response and Cassidy couldn't help but stare. She had heard that laugh before. It was the type that was only born from testing yourself against impossible odds and emerging triumphant. It was a laugh of excitement and danger. It was a laugh that, so far, Cassidy had only ever heard come out of her own mouth.

Aldan expertly maneuvered the craft through the descent. The engine sputtered intermittently, providing a boost forward during their fall that confused Cassidy until she noticed that each sputter corresponded with a flash of light on the lens he wore.

He was hitting invisible checkpoints on their route. Wherever they were headed, and whoever was there waiting for them, must have some of the most advanced security features that Cassidy had ever encountered. She fervently hoped that his cocky attitude was well-earned. She had no desire to see how the security system reacted if they didn't correctly identify themselves.

The engines kicked back in and slowed their descent. Aldan gave a self-satisfied hum and lowered the craft, skimming the tree line close enough that the highest branches swayed with annoyance.

Cassidy wondered if she would have a chance to explore planet-side before returning home. She had never seen trees like this before—they were nothing like the ones that grew outside of the Tellurian government building.

They reminded her of stinger nettles back on Earth. Long branches stretched out of thin spiny trunks toward the sky, but the needles that adorned the deep green leaves looked like claws grasping at the weak sunlight that was filtered by the thick cloud cover. The closer they came, the more easily she could make out large swaths of browned and crumbling vegetation.

"The added cloud coverage from the volcano must make it hard to get around. You're a very good pilot."

When Aldan blinked at her in confusion she clarified. "Back home we have instruments to help us navigate around volcanoes. The additional smoke plumes can be hard to see through."

Aldan shook his head. "We have the technology to navigate through clouds as well. We have to. But this volcano has no plume. That's why it blocks signals so well. Everything is contained within the mountain."

Cassidy eyed the tree line again. "Then why is it so hard for the sunlight to pierce the clouds? The plants are dying."

"Plants are dying all over Telluria." His voice was carefully neutral when he responded, but Cassidy could hear the tinge of control waver when he spoke. "This cloud system stretches across the entire moon. That's why the growing stations you visited are so important for our survival."

His careful words were like a punch to the gut. Her sinking feeling had nothing to do with Aldan landing the craft, and everything to do with the guilt that was blooming in her chest.

Aldan hovered over a small landing strip before

touching down with a thump, depressurizing the cabin and then opening the porthole with the click of a dial.

He swung himself from the hatch with ease and turned to see if she needed any assistance.

Cassidy accepted it and bit back a groan as she balanced on her cramped legs, stretching them once she was back on solid ground.

The area around them was dark and damp. There was no sign of any plant or animal life running through the mud, unlike in the swamps or bogs back on Earth. Here it was impossible for anything to grow underneath the tree canopy.

Aldan gestured ahead of them. At the edge of the landing strip stood a derelict shed—a refueling station was her best guess—the only structure that Cassidy could see around them.

"Cassidy Cane," Aldan's voice seemed thin in the empty air around them, "welcome to the home of the Tellurian Resistance!"

# CHAPTER FIVE

The little shack was lackluster at best. At first Cassidy thought that the tiny building was a joke, and she wondered what she had managed to get herself into by agreeing to the break-out with Aldan. Then, to her immense relief, he'd pushed aside the heavy-looking storage crates with a touch of his wristband.

The metal floor paneling slid across the room and created an opening large enough to display a locked hatch under the floor. Leaning forward, he punched a code into an unlit keypad and was rewarded with a beep from the locking mechanism as the hatch popped open.

"Your security measures are very extensive," she told him as he gestured for her to take the lead into the depths below.

"They have to be. We can't leave anything to chance."

Cassidy grasped the smooth metal rungs of the ladder and let the darkness swallow her. "And your aircraft?"

"Already hidden. The landing platform retracts underground." Aldan flexed his fingers. Cassidy heard a clicking sound, and bright beams of light shot out from the tips of his glove.

Aldan followed after her, locking the entryway above them with ease. He jiggled the handle to make sure that it had closed. She heard the metal floor slide back across the hatch as he joined her in her descent.

Cassidy reached the bottom and eyed the glove with interest. "I've got to get me one of those," she murmured.

Aldan grinned, locating a hidden marker that Cassidy couldn't see and trudging toward it. "I'm sure we have an extra one lying sound somewhere that could find its way into your pocket," he replied, motioning for her to follow him.

She looked around, unable to differentiate between the labyrinth of tunnels that branched out from where they stood, then followed him with a shrug.

The only sound was the shallow scuffing of their footfalls against the packed earth under their boots. The sound of the pinging of the metal pipes disappeared behind them as they went deeper underground.

Aldan swept his hand ahead of them, the lights in his gloves outlining the dark interior of the tunnels and the different paths that stretched endlessly before them. "These were once mining tunnels," he told her, stepping unerringly in a direction with a conviction that left Cassidy baffled. "The mines were abandoned once the volcano became more active. The churning of the core disrupted the mining instruments too severely to be of any use. Wherever melted minerals were dredged up from the inside of the moon didn't agree with the Sublunaries's technology and caused the robots to keep deactivating. So they abandoned the project."

Cassidy noted that his disdain for the Alluvians was a

near-match to how the Alluvians felt about the Tellurians. "Plus the volcano could erupt at any time... right?" Cassidy found that the hum of molten activity was growing louder the deeper they went into the tunnels. She wouldn't want to be trapped here if it decided to blow its top.

Aldan quirked a sardonic half-smile. "Right," he said, but his tone implied that that was never a factor in the decision. He pivoted so abruptly that Cassidy would have collided with him if she hadn't been paying attention. He peered at the opening of a new corridor, then gave a satisfied nod before leading them down it.

Cassidy could see nothing marking the way. "How do you know where to go? Forgive my skepticism, but it seems unlikely that you have the path memorized..." Her voice trailed off in a drawl as a rockslide loomed ahead of them, cutting off their route.

Aldan took a step forward. "I can't tell you all of our secrets, Cassidy Cane," he murmured.

To her immense surprise, he reached out and pressed random rocks in the pile of rubble. There was a change of pitch in the hum around them. He threw a smirk over his shoulder and stepped forward, leaving her gaping as he walked through the rocks and disappeared in front of her.

"You better be dreaming, Cassidy," she muttered to herself, hurrying after him in an attempt to keep up. She held her arms in front of her, expecting the resistance of the stones, but she felt nothing as she walked right through the rock pile. A well-lit tunnel stretched before her on the other side. It was almost like walking through a portal.

Aldan shot her a bemused look. "The light projection remains intact. I just shut off the force shield."

Cassidy schooled her expression. "There never was a cave-in in the tunnel."

"There never was a cave-in in the tunnel," he confirmed her statement, motioning to a large, locked door ahead of them. He took off his glove and held his hand against a lit pad. There was a beep when the scan completed, and a click as the door unlocked at his touch. He swung it open with a dramatic flair and gestured for her to take the lead.

Cautiously, Cassidy stuck her head through the exit and was greeted by the sight of an empty, windowed dome. She stepped forward and, waiting as Aldan secured the door behind them, peered out through the glass before them.

The glass entrance dome was situated above a large room. It jutted out from the top, much like a bay window would on a house, and allowed Cassidy an unobstructed view of everything below her — as well as an unobstructed view of her to everything below her.

Several heads craned upward and stared at her with surprise. Others looked at the string of alarms that stretched across the walls, as if waiting for a sign that they had to spring to action at her presence. The alarm system remained dark and quiet, offering no explanation.

Aldan took up the position next to her. The people below them visibly relaxed, and a wave of tension left the room at the sight of him.

Aldan removed his headband, powering down the lens — the thing that had undoubtedly allowed him to see the hidden markings in the tunnels, and tucked it under his arm. "Cassidy Cane, the Terrorist of Telluria, welcome to the true home of the Tellurian Resistance."

# CHAPTER SIX

Cassidy paced the hallway in agitation. It had been over an hour since Aldan had entered the meeting chamber and she hadn't heard a sound since. She had caught sight of three official-looking Tellurians waiting in the room, scowling at him, before the door was unceremoniously closed in her face. No one had checked on her since.

She ran her hands through her hair, feeling the snarls and tangles that had accumulated from her adventures over the past few days. She used her fingers to comb it out in an attempt to look more presentable, using the hair tie around her wrist to secure her fiery stands when she was finished.

What she wouldn't give to have a shower.

This area of the underground compound seemed newer than the rest. Cassidy found her attention trailing along the walls to where the adjoining concrete tunnels connected at different intervals of the hallway.

"No one said I couldn't explore," she murmured to herself. Tellurian technology continued to surprise her. If she could have some time to herself to analyze it uninterrupted...

The large door opened with an audible strike against the latch plate. An older gentleman stuck his head around the doorframe. Curious lilac eyes met her own. "Cassidy Cane? Please come in." he opened the door in polite invitation.

She offered him a smile. "Thank you," she murmured, inclining her head as she stepped past him into the room...

—and came to an immediate halt when she realized that it looked almost identical to the courtroom where she had tried pleading her case only yesterday.

Cassidy tried not to feel anxious as the door was closed and locked behind her.

*** 

"Cassidy Cane," a soft voice greeted her with surprising warmth.

Cassidy's uneasy sense of deja-vu continued as an elderly woman stepped ahead of the small crowd that had assembled for the meeting. She had the same lavender skin as the Head Magistrate, but her demeanour was softer as her yellow eyes appraised Cassidy with interest.

"My sister was right to alert us to your presence."

Cassidy blinked. "Sister?" She looked to Aldan for confirmation, but he only raised an eyebrow in response. Of course, they would have to have someone on the inside, Cassidy realized. How else would he have known where she was being held?

"I am Taleia," she introduced herself. "Please," she took a step back and gestured to the table and chairs next to her, "take a seat. We have much to discuss."

Cassidy raised her eyebrows but accepted the invitation. She was pleased when, after everyone else took their positions around the meeting table, someone bustled in from a side door with trays of food and drink. Realizing how dry her throat had become, she snagged a glass of water as they were being passed around.

Cassidy almost choked when the bitter liquid hit her throat. While it helped to slake her thirst, it was nothing like the flavour she was expecting. She noticed that everyone around her drank without complaint and wondered if someone had slipped something into her glass.

Small baked loaves were passed around next, and Cassidy's stomach grumbled in response. She took a hesitant bite of the blue-tinged pastry but chewed quickly once the flavour of milled flour hit her tongue. The others dunked their bread in their cups and Cassidy followed suit, noting in surprise that the loaf tempered the strange flavour of the liquid.

"I've read your file," Taleia continued, content to fill the room with speech while the others looked on, "so I understand what your mission was once you came to Telluria... but what I'm interested in is the 'why.'"

Cassidy finished her loaf and wiped her fingers in her pants. "Why what?"

Taleia leaned forward, eyeing Cassidy earnestly. "Why did you conspire with the Sublunaries to sabotage our crops? You seem like a highly educated woman—the opposite of how our government's smear campaign describes you," Cassidy raised her brows at that, but Taleia continued, "so why attack us without provocation?"

Cassidy leaned back, away from Taleia's scrutiny, and took stock of the room around her. Everyone at the table, Aldan included, had given her their undivided attention. Mistrust simmered in some of their pale gazes, some were tinged with anger as they waited for her reply, but despite the unpleasantness of the emotions that hung in the room, no hostility painted the faces that were turned toward her. Just open-minded curiosity.

They were nothing like the Alluvians had led her to believe, and not for the first time since coming to Telluria did Cassidy feel a sinking in her stomach.

She cleared her throat. "I assume by "Sublunaries," you mean the inhabitants of the planet that you orbit?"

Taleia gave a stiff nod. "That is what we call them, yes. You might know them as Alluvian."

Cassidy cocked her head, her mind moving too quickly to realize that her mouth was about to get her into trouble. "But you call them Sublunary? Because they are *sub-par* in relation to Tellurians?"

Taleia's brows shot toward her hairline, but the male sitting next to her interjected before she could. "Because their needs are not more important than the Tellurian's," his voice was a practiced mild rebuke, but his gaze slid to Aldan, as if blaming him for Cassidy's outburst.

Aldan's face colored uncomfortably under the attention of the older gentleman, and he slid down a little in his chair.

"But they are the ones who provide you with food."

"We provide them with food!" The man retorted, his fist banging the table in emphasis loud enough to make everyone jump. "And because of it we are stuck, beholden to them as their greed grows. They withhold technology from us and dictate how we are to live all so that they are able to grow fat on our labour while our own children starve—"

"Their children are starving," Cassidy interjected, her voice low enough to cut through his speech. "They give you the means to feed yourselves and yet you withhold food—"

"Withhold food!" Matching her intensity, the man rose and leaned toward her over the table. "We have done no such thing."

"I've seen the silos—"

"Did you go *in* them?" he sneered. "Did you see how little we've been able to put aside for emergencies? How close we are to starvation? Those silos house the entire moon's food supply!"

Cassidy stared at him, dumbfounded. He was right. Cassidy hadn't even checked on their supply level. She hadn't bothered to validate the Alluvians's story. She had been so preoccupied with saving their children and securing their lung-scanning technology, that she hadn't seen their story for the lie it was. That was before she'd learned that the Alluvians had planned to blow her up instead of coming to her aid, of course. Before Aldan had stepped in and saved her.

Taleia raised her palms to halt the conversation. "That is quite enough, Mycah," she admonished, her voice soft. "Cassidy is our guest and unfamiliar with our customs, and what actually happens on Telluria. Yelling at her will not teach her any faster, nor will it warm her to our cause."

The man, Mycah, had the grace to look abashed and seated himself without another sound.

Cassidy crossed her arms. She watched Mycah, unconvinced, but when his full attention remained focused on Taleia, Cassidy slid her gaze to the woman instead. "And what is your cause, exactly?"

Taleia sat back in her chair. She placed tapered fingertips to her left temple and began to rub it slowly, looking very tired all of a sudden. "What did the Alluvians say to you to convince you to commit your act of sabotage?"

Cassidy weighed her options for her response. Initially she had told the Tellurian Government that she had flown her own vessel to the moon as an independent act of defiance, but with the admission of portals to Aldan earlier...

She looked over and saw that he was the only other person in the room watching her, his yellow eyes unreadable as he waited for her response. Their eyes met and he cocked his head and raised a brow. *Go on*, his expression told her.

She realized there was no help for it. They'd find out eventually. The Tellurian Government was probably already combing the area where they found her. They may have already located the portal system. For all she knew, they were having tea with Gamgee at this very moment.

Cassidy raised a brow back at Aldan and returned her attention to Taleia. "I'll tell you everything you need to know, but first you must do something for me."

Taleia's brows flattened, and Cassidy fought the need to wince. "I don't mean to sound ungrateful," she continued, her voice softer. She had to be careful. She wanted them sympathetic, not offended.

Cassidy cleared her throat. "I really appreciate you getting me out of that cell. Aldan took no small risk, and I am grateful to him for that—but this isn't about me. I have family and friends to think about—a whole planet to protect. I need assurances."

A murmur went through the room at her statement. Taleia sat up straight in her chair at Cassidy's proclamation. "And which planet is that, Cassidy Cane?"

Cassidy placed her hands in her lap to steady herself. She felt an unexpected lump form in her throat at the thought of Earth—her parents and her siblings, and yes, even of Gamgee, who must be wondering where she was as her fake Cancun holiday was past its end.

*Home…*

She cleared her throat. "A planet far away," she said softly, to the curious faces that had turned toward her, "that is unaware of my ignorant trespassing, and of any damage that I may have done. It is innocent, and it deserves to be kept out of whatever ongoing conflict between your two worlds that I seem to have inadvertently put myself in the middle of, and I intend to make sure it remains safe."

"And what do you require to do that?" Taleia probed in the growing silence after Cassidy's impromptu speech.

"Explosives," Cassidy responded without hesitation. Taleia pressed her lips together, and she raised a hand to stem the woman's silent disapproval. "Not weapons—though yours do seem to be much more advanced than anything we have back home. But that's exactly why I need them to stay here. I want an explosive big enough to ensure that once I'm through the portal no one will follow after me. I want to seal it shut."

The murmuring began in earnest when she finished, and Cassidy let them argue among themselves. She didn't have to persuade anyone—she knew she had the upper hand. They needed her more than she needed them. She wanted to get back to Earth as soon as possible, but not if it meant risking the planet. Not if it meant risking her friends. Both the Alluvian and Tellurian technology was far more advanced than anything available on Earth—she couldn't let it follow her back. Spending the rest of her life as a guest of the Tellurian Resistance was the better option, and she knew that they knew she was right.

Her attention turned to Aldan. He remained quiet during the debate that raged around them. His self-satisfied smirk shone like a beacon in the room, and Cassidy wondered how much of her rescue had been his idea, or if he had even had the blessing of the Resistance. Judging by his cat-that-ate-the-canary expression, she had no trouble believing that he had assigned himself a solo mission.

He knew that portals—or something like them—existed. She had been nothing but the pawn in a long-standing game between the two planets that happened to arrive with the proof. Lucky her.

Taleia also noticed Aldan's expression and frowned. She placed her palms on the table. It was an understated move that generated no noise, yet the entirety of the table fell silent with the small gesture. All eyes turned to the woman seated at the head of the table, and Cassidy couldn't help but feel impressed at the quiet power that the woman held over the group.

Taleia met Aldan's gaze until he began to fidget under her attention. "We will speak about this later," she informed him. "Privately."

Aldan had the grace to look abashed. "Yes, Grandmother."

Cassidy didn't have time to react. Taleia's yellow gaze slid to her, commanding Cassidy's full attention. The two women stared at each other, silent, until Taleia returned her fingers to her forehead with a sigh. "Portals," she muttered to herself, almost inaudibly, resuming the circular rubbing against her temple as the room held its breath.

"The Council has heard your request, Cassidy Cane. And while we will debate the merits of the situation later, I want the whole story from the beginning. All of it. Leave nothing out. We will then evaluate our next moves accordingly."

Taleia straightened her spine and waited for any rebuttal, but no one interjected. The Council was letting her run with it, and for that Cassidy was unsure if she was grateful or apprehensive.

"You've made a fine mess for Telluria, Cassidy Cane. Now it's time for us to figure out how to best clean it up."

Cassidy felt her stomach drop. Apprehensive... Definitely apprehensive.

Taleia lifted the large pitcher of water and poured a generous glass, sliding it to Cassidy. She smirked, but not unkindly. "Now, if you please. From the beginning."

# CHAPTER SEVEN

Cassidy took another sip of the tepid water, rolling the unfamiliar flavour over her tongue. There were minerals in it she couldn't identify—not surprising, since she was on a different planet—and while it didn't taste *bad*, it certainly didn't quench her thirst like she was used to. It wasn't as crisp as the water she was used to drinking on Earth. None of the others seemed to have the same feelings about it as she did, so she said nothing. There was much that she didn't know about Telluria, and so far, she was only beginning to scratch the surface of it.

They had gone over everything twice now. The first time she had told the story without interruption. She had only briefly touched on the backstory of her exploring different worlds through the portals with Gamgee—she had left him completely out of it—and let them think that it was of her own accord that she was here. The last thing she needed was to incite a panic that Earth's government would storm through the moon looking for her if she didn't return on time. Glossing over unnecessary Earth information, she began the story in earnest when she arrived on Alluvia. She described the desert-like conditions that she encountered outside of the cave-system. After all of the archaeological digs that she had taken part in in her lifetime, Cassidy was no stranger to surviving in deserts, but the rapt expressions of those around her reminded her of the wonder that she had first experienced when face-to-face with a terrain of sand and sky and a harsh sun beating down on her.

"I've heard the Alluvians describe their planet before, but I never truly believed what they were saying," one of the councilmen had said in a hushed tone. The others around him shushed him into silence.

That was the only interruption the first time through. Unsurprisingly, they made her tell it again. This time, they interrupted her to ask questions, clarifying different parts of her story and taking notes. She was unsure if it was for their own information, or if it was a test on the validity of her story, but eventually they seemed satisfied and had stopped asking questions. Most had excused themselves and rushed from the council chambers without a backward glance.

Cassidy sipped her water again, enjoying the rest no matter how brief. She became acutely aware that she had not slept in some time and could feel the exhaustion tugging at the corners of her senses as she fought to remain alert in her chair.

Aldan remained. As did Taleia.

"If what you say is true," Taleia began, holding up a hand to deflect any offense that her words may have caused but Cassidy just shrugged, she was too tired to be offended at this point, "then the Alluvians are in a much worse position than we are."

Aldan cocked his head. He folded his legs under him in the chair and leaned forward. "How so? They are not the ones trapped on their planet."

"They are, but for different reasons," his grandmother disagreed with a shake of her head. "And they are stuck not being able to use their planet. We always thought that the scattered visitor wore their breathing equipment on Telluria because of our atmosphere, but if what Cassidy says is true..." Cassidy waved her hand to show that she again took no offense with Taleia's doubt, "they are only capable of surviving in their domes without them."

Aldan slapped the table in front of him in exasperation, causing Cassidy to twitch in her tired state. "That doesn't excuse them ruining our food supply and endangering Tellurian lives!"

He hushed his tone part way through with a look from Taleia, and she pressed her lips together in thought. "No, it certainly does not."

"Why can't the Alluvians grow their own food?" Cassidy asked, draining her glass of the remaining water. "Wouldn't it be easier for them to set up their own growing stations instead of shipping the fertilizer up here to use in yours?"

Aldan snorted and Taleia shook her head. "It's not a fertilizer—though I assume the properties are similar. It's a growing agent. It's synthetic enzymes that transform the soil to make it more receptive to the crops we sow so that it's possible to grow them."

Cassidy blinked in surprise. It made sense. If the outside vegetation—or lack thereof, depending on what part of the planet she was located on—was any indication of the growing environment, nothing here would be edible for humanoids. "That's amazing!"

Taleia dipped her head in a nod.

"The Alluvians destroyed their planet—the soil, the water —the very air they breathe is poison. It's impossible to grow anything in that environment," Aldan expanded with a shrug. "They don't have enough resources to use space in their domes."

"So it's easier to set up proper lighting and ship this chemical agent here as opposed to shipping everything the planet would need to grow their own supplies," Cassidy murmured. She thought back to the transport ship she had used and had to agree. The sheer volume of water and soil that would constantly have to be harvested from the moon seemed like an impossible task for the tiny ship. The Alluvians already treated their own drinking water, but the amount that would be needed to grow their own food would be impossible.

"Easier, but not easy." Taleia sighed. "The ground needs pre-treating. Lights need to be created—no doubt you've noticed our cloudy atmosphere—irrigation systems need to be created and installed… It's doable with help from the Alluvian government, but it can take years just to get the supplies here. Chuga takes a massive amount of resources to grow."

"They don't have that kind of time."

When the Tellurians blinked at her, Cassidy cleared her throat. "I've seen their medical scans… I think they need more Chuga because their deficiencies are getting worse. Their children's survival is in danger. Now. Some of them may not last the current growing season."

The last part came out in a whisper, and both Taleia and Aldan's expressions became grave.

"But why ship the growing agent? Why not just get you to create it here?" Cassidy knew that pollution was a concern for the planet, so why would they knowingly contribute to it when they could just as easily create it on Telluria? Even on Earth, the pollution created by synthetic fertilizers was concerning. She could only imagine that creating something that essentially rewrote the nutritional compounds of the soil itself must also be high on that list.

Aldan snorted, his face an expression of disdain. "They won't tell us how to make it."

Cassidy blinked at him.

She looked at Taleia who gave a quick nod. "They worry that if Tellurians knew how to create the agent, we would then look for compensation for the food—an arrangement they are willing to avoid at all costs."

Cassidy frowned. "And if you can't make it—"

"—Then we have no control over our own food supply." Aldan finished. "They want to keep us fully dependent upon them. Even the knowledge of space travel is guarded with jealousy. Only their robots function as mechanics should something go wrong during a transport run."

Cassidy frowned and tapped her fingers on the table. It was the only sound in the vast room before she stilled. "I'm sorry," she told them, her shoulders slumping, "for the part I played, as ignorant as I was about it. Your people are in danger and it's all my fault."

The silence grew between them until Taleia spoke.

"Then make it right," she told her, her voice soft. "Fix the mistake that you made."

Cassidy stretched out her hands. "How?"

"Take us to your portal. Lead our team onto the Alluvial home world so that we may replenish what was destroyed." Taleia reached out to take Cassidy's hands in her own. "Lead our people to freedom, Cassidy Cane. We can't do it without you."

# CHAPTER EIGHT

Aldan led the way through a set of double doors. The smell of cooking food wafted toward them, causing Cassidy's stomach to growl in response. She couldn't remember the last time she had eaten a full meal.

She trailed him into the mess hall and stood next to him in the service queue, noting how the room resembled any of the dozens of cafeterias that she had been in on Earth.

"Tell me about the Alluvian facility," Aldan probed, scanning the room with a thoughtful expression on his face.

Cassidy followed his gaze and was unsurprised to find that most of the attention in the room was fixated on her. Some averted their eyes, but others stared openly at her, meeting her gaze in a way that made her grateful for Aldan's company in the large room. Their expressions hovered between curiosity and hostility, and Cassidy decided that she didn't want to give them the chance to explore either.

"*Terrorist*," she heard someone hiss behind her, and she twisted to see a small group of diners exit the room.

Aldan watched her; his brows raised as he waited for her response. Cassidy pulled her attention back to their conversation as best she could. "Similar to this, actually."

Aldan's expression turned to disbelief, so she continued.

"I mean, the technology is more advanced, yes. But the basic structure is similar. The major difference is that their buildings are above ground. They are also air-tight where they rise above the dome."

Aldan snorted as they moved up in the line. Cassidy noticed that no one joined it behind them. "They have no choice but to keep out the air," Aldan growled, his posture becoming tense. "Their air is poison. *They* are poison. And now they seek to spread that poison to Telluria? I will not allow it."

Cassidy pursed her lips at his bravado. "What they did—what they tricked me into doing—was despicable, yes. But I don't think greed or hatred was the motivator. I think it was fear." Aldan slid his gaze toward her, so she continued. "Their population is still growing. They're at a standstill with what they can do on Alluvia, but they're unable to leave. Physiologically, they can't survive in your atmosphere any easier than they can in theirs. They need resources and they need them now."

"That's no excuse to endanger us," Aldan shot back, stepping forward with such force that his boot stomped on the floor before he could control himself.

"You're right," Cassidy agreed. Those closest to them were casting hard looks in her direction. "There's no excuse for that. But sometimes, I think, when you have to choose between the certain hardship of your loved ones and a potential one for those you have never met, every-one tends to embrace the former rather than the latter. It's definitely not a situation I envy them being in."

Aldan's posture relaxed and he looked at her with in-terest.

Cassidy took the opportunity to ask a question that was bugging her. "Why destroy your supplies, though? Surely you would just replace them?"

"We can't eat the chuga. It's poison to us. Our bodies have adapted to needing less vitamin D because of our atmosphere, so we are unable to filter out the extra vita-mins and our organs shut down. I suspect the plan was to leverage our agent as payment for the extra Chuga, while negotiating for more fields at the expense of our own growing space."

"Oh."

The line moved forward and Aldan was next for the servers. He pressed a code into the keypad which hummed in response. There was a soft churning, the sound of mech-anized wheels behind the scenes, then everything halted with a cheery *ding!* that caused Cassidy to stifle a grin. A thin metal door rolled up and two serving trays slid for-ward onto the small shelf.

Aldan handed the first one to Cassidy before taking his own and leading the way to a pair of vacant chairs.

Cassidy set her metal tray on the cafeteria table and immediately heard the scraping of chairs around her. She watched as some of the Tellurians closest to her aban-doned their meals to exit the mess, muttering between themselves.

Cassidy swung herself into her seat and sniffed at her

clothing. "Do they find my smell offensive?"

Aldan sat across from her and took a long drink of water before answering. "I think it's your 'Tellurian Terrorist' title that they find offensive, if anything."

Cassidy winced, and he shot her a sympathetic look before tucking into his food. She picked up a pronged utensil and attempted to do the same.

Almost everything on the tray was tinged with blue. Several types of oddly-shaped vegetables—something that she would have called prehistoric carrots if she were back on Earth—were nestled in the pockets of the dish. Long thin grains, reminiscent of rice, filled a bowl and smelled faintly of salt and herbs. Even the tea had a blue tinge to it.

The only thing spared from the color was the bland-looking white fish that still rested on its skewers. Without hesitation, Cassidy began to unceremoniously shove the grilled fish into her mouth.

"It must be hard to sustain wildlife on your moon," she said after eating half of it, breaking the silence.

Aldan pursed his lips, spoon hovering in the air with his next bite of food. He cocked his head as if he had never considered it. "Yes, and no," he replied after a moment's thought. "Fish are easy. Low-light plants grow in our waters, which allow support for them as well as insects. The larger meat sources are much more complicated."

"Such as the vecas?"

Aldan nodded. "The Alluvians have found a way to supplement and synthesize the vecas's food supply within their enclosures, allowing them to graze. It is not something that we grow here."

Cassidy chewed her fish. That made sense. It was easier to allot space and resources for grass in comparison to an entire population's food supply.

"Are there any natural predators?"

"Not on land." When she raised her eyebrows, he grinned. "We get the odd fisher's tale, for sure. And sometimes larger beasts wash up on shore. But so far, no one's ever been able to catch one."

Cassidy nodded and popped a shriveled root vegetable into her mouth. "It took us a very long time on Earth before we were able to capture large sea creatures."

Aldan's yellow eyes became curious. "You'll have to take me some time."

"To Earth?"

"Yes…. Tell me about it?"

Cassidy tilted her head. "A question for a question," she offered, taking a sip of her drink.

Aldan paused his eating at her serious expression. "Very well," he agreed, solemnly.

Cassidy cleared her throat. "Why did you help me?" When he looked surprised, she clarified. "After I sabotaged the irrigation system. You knew what I had done, and yet you helped me to escape. Why?"

Aldan gave a shrug. It was meant to come off as impish, but he didn't quite hit the mark. "We'd intercepted a communication from the Alluvian government warning us of an alien ship in orbit around their planet. It piqued my interest." When Cassidy blinked in surprise he continued. "They don't know how much our sensors have advanced in the past few years. I knew that there was no ship in orbit. Just as I knew there was no ship present when you were arrested upon your return." Realization clanged through Cassidy. No wonder he had been watching for her return—he had already had suspicions about the portals. "And I knew a transport vessel was arriving when we received the warning. The timing was too coincidental. I assumed they were setting up a scapegoat. And I know all too well what the government does to criminals."

His voice was low with the last sentence. Cassidy felt her mouth go dry and took a sip of her drink to try and ease it. She had already contaminated the irrigation system when Aldan had caught up with her, and even knowing what she had done he had saved her anyway.

Cassidy swallowed. "Thank you." Her voice came out hoarse despite her best efforts. It was too simple a thing to say to someone who had done so much for her.

Aldan shrugged off her thanks. "I should be thanking you."

"Thanking me?"

Aldan smirked and leaned forward. "I love it when my interest is piqued."

Cassidy felt her cheeks redden under the weight of his stare. She used the pronged utensil to shove another piece of the crispy fish into her mouth. "What would you like to know about Earth?"

*** 

A light *bump* jostled Cassidy from sleep. Sharpening her senses against the haze in her mind she opened her eyes, only to be greeted by the back of Aldan's head from the pilot's chair. He powered down the engines. "You gonna make it?"

"I'll do my best," she quipped, a huge yawn splitting her face as she stretched in her seat.

Aldan grinned, and Cassidy felt her face redden at his response.

The porthole whooshed open, and Aldan laughed as he climbed through it with ease. Cassidy followed suit, after she disengaged her safety straps, vaulting herself after him to the ground below.

They were inside a massive mountain crater.

The distinct pattern of the rock was familiar. Cassidy toed at the glassy surface before inspecting the area around them, assessing where Aldan had set down the aircraft. There was no doubt that she was back at the cave system that housed the portals, but their access to the site had come from the air. The open sky that currently stretched above her was not visible from the underground caverns where she'd arrived.

The sound of approaching footfalls made her freeze, and Cassidy turned her attention to Aldan to check on his status.

Aldan ran his fingers through his hair and gave her a cocky grin. "You didn't think we were the only ones here, did you?"

Cassidy said nothing, letting her glare do all the talking.

Aldan pressed his lips together to stifle a laugh.

A pair of Tellurians came into view from the other side of the aircraft. Cassidy was dismayed to see that they wore a uniform similar to the guards from the Government building.

They saluted Aldan before adopting a wide-legged

stance. The woman, the closest soldier to them, rested her hand on the hilt of her holstered weapon while casually keeping Cassidy in her sights.

Aldan assessed the woman, then slid his gaze to the man. "Anything to report?" There was no trace of the usual warmth in his voice.

"Everything is ready on our end, sir. We synthesized fake rockslides and cave-ins to deter the government's search parties from finding the entrance to the caves."

Aldan frowned. "Search parties already? That was fast."

"Yes sir," the woman replied. "It seems they are looking for the missing fugitive and assume she will be returning to the place of capture."

It took Cassidy a moment to realize that the woman's disdain was directed at her. She opened her mouth to reply in kind, but Aldan cut her off before she had the chance.

"Any other activity to report?" When they shook their heads, Aldan nodded. "Very good. I want regular updates—regardless if there's anything to report or not. Keep a low profile. I don't want anyone engaging with the other forces without my say-so. Understood?" He looked satisfied when they nodded. "Dismissed,"

They saluted again and, without so much as a glance to Cassidy, returned to their posts.

"You're military," she said to Aldan, her question coming out as a statement. No wonder he knew what the government did to criminals.

"Ex-military," he corrected, rolling his shoulders. "You didn't think I got by on my rugged good looks, did you?"

He laughed when she gaped at him and strolled over to a projector terminal, activating the device that would hide the base from aerial view.

Ignoring the warmth in her cheeks, Cassidy walked in the opposite direction, curiosity directing her to trudge further into their base of operations. She was careful to avoid the stationed soldiers, opting instead for the glassy paths that snaked deeper into the earth. Small points of light, tiny glowing rocks that were scattered haphazardly along the floors of the tunnels, illuminated the paths like flickering stars in the darkness. It wasn't enough for her to see what was ahead, but they were an excellent way to show where the Tellurians had already been.

Aldan came to stand behind her. "Light markers," he said, nodding to the path ahead. "We can turn them off when necessary, so that they blend into their surroundings."

"Genius," Cassidy replied. "Hansel and Gretel would have had a much easier time with things if they'd used glowing breadcrumbs."

Aldan looked confused. "Did your soldiers deploy without proper reconnaissance gear for their mission?"

Cassidy surprised herself by laughing. The soft sound erupting from her as she dismissed her comment with a wave of her hand. "Something like that." Of course, he wouldn't know Earth fables.

Inspecting the area around them, she tapped her fingers against the cool wall with a soft hum.

"Problem?" Aldan asked in response to the frown that spread across her face.

Cassidy dropped her hand. "I don't know where the

entrance is."

Aldan raised his brows. "Pardon?"

Cassidy gestured around them. "We're up too high. I arrived underground; in a cave that sloped up to the surface. I didn't come into an open-air cavern such as this."

Aldan's frown mirrored her own. "This is the only opening our scout vessels could find that offered us a high enough vantage point against possible attack."

Cassidy cocked her head. "Scout vessels? *Flying* scout vessels...?"

A flicker of exasperation played across Aldan's face, and he pinched the bridge of his nose. "...Which are completely unhelpful if you were found on the ground and not in the air." Aldan pursed his lips in thought, walking slowly back toward the large, illuminated cavern where his aircraft rested, commanding the space of the barren room around it. Barren except for the military supply crates that were grouped together next to the soldiers that were farthest away from the entrance.

"You said that you were picked up by a government patrol car?" he asked, slowing his steps until he became still. When Cassidy nodded, he looked thoughtful. "It will take months for us to explore the entire cave system. The mountains span along the road for a day's drive, and the tunnels stretch between them. But if you could remember a landmark of some sort from where they found you..."

Cassidy racked her brain, sifting through everything that had happened in the past few days. "Not where they found me, no," the whole area had been dried red earth with large rocks and little vegetation, "but before that, yes!" Cassidy felt her heartbeat speed up as she thought back. "There was a section of the road that had cliffs on both sides. The mountain had been blasted in order to create the road. It was the only section like that that I encountered."

"I know exactly where that is," he mused, and Cassidy felt a surge of relief as he continued "but the question is, how do we get down there without being noticed? Patrols are already looking for you."

Cassidy cast her gaze around the cavern again, stopping when her eyes alighted on the tactical gear. She nodded to the harnesses that were stacked next to large coils of thick, woven rope. "How are you at cave rappelling?"

Aldan grinned, and the glint in his eye caused the tips of her fingers to tingle in response.

# CHAPTER NINE

Cassidy peered over the lip of the cliff into the darkness below. Her headlamp illuminated a short distance of the open air in front of her, but it did little to assist the yawning descent she was faced with.

It had taken them hours to get this far—tracking their way through an underground labyrinth of paths to get down to where they were now. Several times they had to reclimb a cliff and skirt their way to another opening when they could find no exits from their current plateau.

"Do you see it?" Aldan's voice seemed far away in consuming darkness. The only indication that she was not alone was the flickering of his headlamp as he searched the area.

Cassidy combed the darkness with her gaze until she found the light marker that he tossed into the chasm. "Found it."

"Distance?"

"About 40 feet, give or take."

She heard him grunt in acknowledgement as he did a mental calculation to the Tellurian unit of measurement.

"Sounds great."

"Great!" And, without another moment's hesitation, Cassidy tipped herself over the edge of the rock face and into the gaping chasm below.

"Cassidy!" Aldan yelped, and she could see the light ring of his headlamp pitch forward in an attempt to catch her.

Laughter bubbled out of her as she fell through the darkness. She let the loose, bottom section of the rope run across the palm of her hand, watching the size of the light marker grow at an almost alarming rate as she barrelled toward it. She waited until she judged herself close enough, then activated the Tellurian gripping gloves that Aldan had given her to wear.

Her descent came to an immediate halt as the force shields from the gloves latched onto the thick rope with a sharp jerk. Cassidy grunted at the strain in her arms from the sudden stop. Deactivating the gloves, she slid the remaining ten feet down to rope to the solid rock below.

She heard a thud as Aldan landed several feet away from her. "Are you insane?" he demanded, flustered.

"Sometimes," she acknowledged in a too-cheery tone. Aldan muttered to himself under his breath as he unhooked his harness from the rope with more force than was necessary.

Cassidy unclipped herself and walked the few feet to pick up the light marker. Holding it, she tapped a dial on the back of her glove and felt a small twinge of satisfaction when the fist-sized stone went dark.

They looked around. Their light beams converged at an opening in the rock wall, and Aldan made a noise of satisfaction.

As one, they left their ropes hanging and walked toward the opening across the plateau. "With any luck, this should lead us to the surface," Aldan said in a hushed tone, peering into the dark passageway when they reached it. He tapped his glove and used the illumination from his fingers to scour the darkness.

"It's in the right direction. And it slopes up," Cassidy offered helpfully, eyeing where the wall joined the floor of the tunnel.

Aldan snorted. "Barely."

She took a few steps forward. "It's the best we've got... unless you'd rather climb back up the cliff and look for something else?" She turned back for the last part and was rewarded when he grumbled under his breath and strode past her.

Grinning, she followed him. They travelled in silence for several minutes, the only noise was the scattered water droplets that fell from the rock above them. After a while, the tunnel veered up at a sharp angle. Cassidy, who had been enjoying the chance to stretch her legs with the hike, cursed her previous optimism as she felt a dull burning in her thighs as she attempted to keep up with Aldan's determined pace. She couldn't tell if his hurried stride was for her benefit or his, but she refused to ask him to slow down as they puffed their way toward the surface.

A distant rumbling caused Aldan to snap to attention, halting in his tracks.

Cassidy lurched her body to the side to avoid him, nearly stumbling in her haste. "What—"

"Shh!" He lifted an illuminated finger to his lips.

Biting back a retort, she remained motionless while

Aldan switched off their lights with his gloves. Their head lamps dimmed, and they were plunged into darkness.

Cassidy could see the outline of his form without their equipment. They were close to the surface.

The rumbling became louder. They both looked up as the vibrations shook the ground above them, knocking loose small rocks that rained down around them haphazardly, bouncing between their boots. Aldan shimmied out of his harness and left it and his shoulder pack fall to the ground with a dull thud. Whipping off his overcoat, he gave it a flick and Cassidy was surprised to see that the material snapped into a thin shield that he immediately held over them.

"Patrol vehicles," Aldan whispered over the rumbling.

Huddled together in the darkness, Cassidy was acutely aware of their shoulders touching, and his warm breath against her cheek. Ignoring it, she eyed the trembling rock face above them as the automobiles drove past. They waited in the silence for several minutes before they dared to move. "We must be under the road," Cassidy said, turning. She stopped abruptly, her face inches from his own where he watched her in the dim light.

She felt heat rise to her cheeks, and the tingling feeling in the tips of her fingers returned, but it wasn't from excitement.

Aldan cleared his throat and snapped down the shield, waving it back into an overcoat. He switched their headlamps back on. "Let's look for an opening," his voice was gruff as he stuffed his harness into his pack and continued up the underground slope.

Cassidy blinked. Rubbing her hands against her legs, she squared her shoulders and followed after him.

She didn't have far to go. There was a slight bend in the tunnel, then a solid rock wall. She assessed the boulders that obstructed their exit to the surface.

"That seems problematic." Cassidy fought the urge to wince when her voice came out more bitter than intended, but she was rewarded when the side of Aldan's mouth quirked up in a smile. "Suggestions?"

Aldan tapped against the rock wall in several places and huffed. "Well, it's not a projection... that means things are about to get loud." He set his backpack on the ground and rummaged inside. He pulled out a small grey blob and jerked his head back the way they came. "Hunker down and get ready to run. We're about to get some unwanted attention."

Cassidy jogged back the way they came, using the bend in the path to shield herself from the impending blast. She covered her ears just as a small explosion rocked the area, sending mid-sized boulders rolling past her from the obstruction.

"Aldan!" she called, rushing forward when he didn't join her. She found him lying on the ground a few feet from the blasting site. He opened his eyes at the sound of her voice and groaned, extending his hand. She grabbed it and pulled him into a standing position.

"That new clay explosive is powerful stuff," he dusted off his pants and made a show of checking that all of his fingers were still attached. "Let's go," he said, when satisfied. "That explosion is certainly going to grab their attention."

Cassidy nodded and took the lead, shifting several of the smaller stones out of the way. Light from the outside world began to filter in through the cracks. She redoubled her efforts, digging at the stones and pushing them out of the way behind her in a small pile. Aldan joined in next to her.

The opening became wide enough to squeeze though. Cassidy pushed herself through the small opening, twisting her body to fit the small space as she climbed around the boulders that were too heavy to move. Once free, she stood a moment to appreciate the warm sun on her face and the fresh breeze in her hair.

"Here," Aldan hissed behind her. She grabbed his offered pack and slung it over a shoulder while he crawled through the opening. She felt better for wearing it. She didn't realize how much she had been missing hers since the Tellurian government had confiscated it. He grinned as he stepped onto the dark red clay of the moon's surface.

He shielded his eyes with a hand and surveyed the area. "Perfect. This is exactly where I wanted to be."

Cassidy rolled her eyes at his smug tone but said nothing.

"You should have come out of the portal around here," he told her, his eyes dragging along the road that cut diagonally in front of them through the outcropping of the rocky mountain. "Now, we just have to determine the direction you..."

Cassidy turned her attention to him when he trailed off. He was peering into the distance, head cocked as if listening for something. "Aldan? What is it?"

He shushed her and remained motionless.

Cassidy stepped around him and strained her eyes to see what he was looking at. She saw nothing but an empty stretch of road that dipped into the horizon. She frowned and was about to open her mouth to admonish him for shushing her, but then movement caught her eye. A cloud of red dust had formed in the distance, and it was growing fast. She watched it, letting her senses focus as it spread across the road and came toward them. Her ears picked up on the muted rumblings of an approaching engine before her feet felt them.

The patrol had heard the explosion, and they were coming to investigate.

Aldan swore under his breath. "We've got to move. Now."

As one, they ran across the road, putting as much distance between them and the obvious blast site as quickly as possible. They threw themselves behind a rocky outcropping while looking for the best place to climb.

Aldan swore again. "The ropes are still hanging where we left them."

"Alert the camp," Cassidy told him. It would take hours for the officers to backtrack through the tunnels to where they had started, possibly even days if they could do it at all, but there was no need to risk it. "I'll look for a place to hide."

Aldan touched the communicator that he wore in his ear while Cassidy scrambled along the base of the ridge to look for a place for them to hide.

Cassidy hurried ahead, scouting for a cave they could duck into when something caught her eye. A small footprint, shrunken into the clay-like ground, led away from the wall of rock and toward the road. Cassidy recognized it as her own from when she originally squeezed out of the cave system into the dark night of Telluria.

"Aldan!"

Aldan jerked his head toward her at her shout. Tapping his earpiece to finish his transmission, he sprinted toward her, nimbly weaving around the rocky outcroppings in an attempt to reach her before the vehicles arrived.

"You found it?" he asked, barely winded as he reached the edge of the footprint. When she nodded, he slid sideways through the opening, extending a hand to help her in after him. "Lead the way." he told her, his voice soft in the small space.

Cassidy nodded and squeezed past him. Retracing her steps with ease, they strode deeper into the mountain.

The rumbling behind them became louder and Cassidy quickened her pace. The scout teams were almost at the entrance to the tunnel.

They arrived at a fork in the road that Cassidy didn't remember, and Aldan collided with her when she paused without warning to inspect it. "What's wrong?"

"This wasn't here last time." She swept her light between the paths that branched off in different directions.

"I thought you said this was the entrance..."

"It is. This is the way I came out."

She could see him frown as he raked his gaze along the walls around them. He squinted, as if trying to make something out. "I don't think there are any projections present..."

The rumbling grew louder. Cassidy felt her heart

speed up as the vehicles came to a halt in front of the hidden entrance. To her surprise, Aldan stepped toward her and gripped her shoulders. With the slightest push of his fingers, he directed her to turn and face the way they came, then pulled her so she took several steps back.

They stood without moving. Cassidy was aware of the light pressure of his fingertips against the sides of her shoulders, and the sounds of the soldiers' boots hitting the ground outside. "Look again," he told her, his voice calming the distractions around them.

The low light through the tiny entrance illuminated the way that she had taken last time. When she'd stumbled from the side-tunnel, connecting with the main one that led to the exit.

Of course, there was no fork in the road. It had been behind her when she arrived. She hadn't noticed the transition because of the number the portal had done on her vision.

"I must really be tired," she muttered with a sigh, taking a step into the tunnel on their now-left.

Aldan chuckled and relieved her of the pack, rummaging in it and pulling out one of the projection shield devices that Cassidy recognized from the underground base. "Go ahead and find the portal. I'll buy us some time," he told her, attaching the device to the outside corner.

Cassidy nodded. She had only travelled several steps before the air around her thickened and she felt the familiar pull of the portal.

Not every portal felt the same. Many didn't offer any warning, so Cassidy was relieved that she was able to find this one with relative ease.

The sound of shouting interrupted her thoughts. A small explosion caused her to stumble, and she heard Aldan curse behind her. The soldiers had blown apart the opening of the tunnel and were heading toward them.

"Run," he told her, as the force shield flickered to life. The projection knit along itself from the rock wall and into the air between them. "I'll distract them while the shield forms. The others in the Resistance will find you. You must get more of the growing agent—"

"Not without you," she interrupted, dismissing his plan of self-sacrifice. Lurching forward, she grabbed his arm and yanked him toward her with all her strength.

They lost their footing and stumbled backward.

The projection completely obstructed the entrance to the tunnel. Even as she felt the air thicken around them, as they fell backward into the portal, Cassidy hoped that it had formed in time to throw the search party off their path.

# CHAPTER TEN

Cassidy grunted as her back slammed into the ground. Above her, Aldan caught himself as he fell on top of her, a grunt escaping his lips with the sudden exertion.

They paused there a moment, staring at each other. His eyes were wide with the shock at the sensation of being transported through a portal.

Snapping out of it, he scrambled to his feet, offering her his hand. "Are you okay?" he asked, his headlamp sputtering as he checked her over.

She accepted his help and he pulled her to her feet with ease. "I'm fine. You?" When he nodded, she exhaled in relief. Their pursuers had not followed them through the portal, so she could only assume that the force shield had activated in time.

His expression of relief turned into annoyance. "That was a foolish thing to do."

"Nonsense. I'm never foolish." Cassidy bit back a grin at the glare he shot her. "Besides, I can't get around Alluvia without you."

He snorted, looking mollified, then gestured ahead of them. "After you."

Cassidy strolled ahead, noting the familiarity of the tunnel as she unhooked her climbing harness. This was going to be easier than she thought.

Sunlight bounced off the shiny walls of the cave that widened at the end of the tunnel, reflecting on the glass-like rock that had formed around the portal. She wondered momentarily which came first—the cave or the portal—and made a note to bring the question up with Gamgee when she returned home.

*Home...*

The acrid chemical smell of the atmosphere invaded her senses. It started as a tingle in her nose, then crept down her throat the longer she continued to breathe it in.

Behind her, Aldan started to cough.

"Welcome to Alluvia," she murmured, stepping from the dark cave into the harsh light of the toxic sun.

\*\*\*

The acrid smell of chemicals snaked its way up her nose and down her throat, causing her to cough as she spoke. Vinegar and rotting vegetation. She hadn't missed that combination. "Now what?"

Aldan's reaction to the smell was worse. He was very obviously trying not to gag as he surveyed the area around them with watering eyes. "Now we wait for our underground operative to make contact," Aldan told her, his voice straining with the effort of suppressing a cough.

Cassidy didn't know if it was his heightened senses, or the fact that his planet was virtually pollution-free, that was giving him such a hard time transitioning to the new atmosphere, but she knew that he had to get inside somewhere—and soon.

"C'mon," Cassidy zipped her coat up and tucked her nose under the collar. She nodded when Aldan followed suit and zipped his collar up over the lower-half of his face. "The dome is up ahead. Let's get you out of the atmosphere."

Slipping into the dome proved easier this time around. Cassidy had led them around to the back of the rock dome, returning to the exit which didn't have the sensors at the front that had alerted the Alluvians to her original arrival and had caused them to launch the automated vehicle that had picked her up. She could only assume that the lack of security was because of the proximity to the other domes that connected in that area.

Cassidy tucked her flaming red hair under a hat—her colouring was closer to the Alluvian's than Aldan's, but her hair would certainly give away the difference—and Aldan paused to smear a pale pigment all over his face. It wasn't quite strong enough, but he could pass for Alluvian so long as no one looked too closely. She held her breath, and the two slipped into the market and joined the crowd of the citizens who were casually strolling between the yellow-orange buildings of the dome.

"Must be lunch time," Cassidy muttered, reminded of the way the campus courtyards filled between classes back on Earth.

The scent of cooking food assaulted their senses, and as one they turned toward the source. A small stand, something akin to a permanent food truck, stood in front of an open-air cooking pit, where the source of the delicious smells was wafting toward them from the automated rotisserie.

Aldan pulled several coins out of his breast pocket and clinked them together in his palm. "In the meantime..."

Cassidy didn't bother asking where he had secured the Alluvian currency. One of his Resistance contacts likely slipped it into transport shipment. Instead, she ordered for them by pointing at the pictured squares on the menu, choosing the combos that were displayed on the beaten plastic sign. Aldan kept his eyes downcast, avoiding meeting the worker's gaze so that his eye colour would not be noticed.

When they received the food, Aldan led the way to an outdoor seating area. He looked as exhausted as she felt, and Cassidy realized that it had been countless hours since either of them had rested.

They ate the food in silence while Aldan assessed the area.

The courtyard was unchanged since her last visit. The red rock of the dome, fortified by the same material she had witnessed a few days ago in the lab, sheltered the Alluvians from their toxic environment. She watched as Aldan ran his gaze up the storeys of yellow buildings to where their heights disappeared against the protection of the dome. Cassidy dragged her gaze to the tunnel that led to the formal garden, and spent a wistful moment wishing she could show Aldan the beautiful trees that grew there. Giving herself a shake, she returned her attention to the space around them.

The hairs on the back of Cassidy's neck prickled. She rubbed at them, looking for the source. There was no wind in this controlled environment, so something else must be causing it.

Her eyes fell on a man seated outside a cafe. He was dressed in the same red clothing that many of the Alluvian's wore, his close-clipped shock of bright orange hair standing out against the red rock that surrounded them. The color was so bright it was almost comical, and it clashed horribly with the red he wore. He was slowly sipping on a hot beverage, looking all the world like a relaxed Earth college student, but the intensity in which he surveyed his surroundings sent a tingle down Cassidy's spine.

"You gonna finish that?" Aldan eyed her half-eaten food. His plate looked as though it had been licked clean, and Cassidy remembered that—other than fish—meat was considered a luxury on Telluria.

"Depends," she countered, pulling her attention back to their table. She turned her body so that the man couldn't see her face. "Can you eat and walk?"

Aldan grinned. "Of course. I'm very accomplished." They rose and he piled her leftover meat onto a square bun with ease. Cassidy gathered the plates and disposed of them in a waste reciprocal as they walked past.

"The building you want is up ahead," she murmured, moving close to him in the public space. She didn't know what the workweek was like—or if they even had a workweek—so she tried her best to emulate the people around her, while also keeping their conversation low enough to avoid any possible eavesdropping.

They had hidden their coloring to the best of their abilities, but there was no need to draw any unnecessary attention.

"Last time you were there you had an escort, yes?" Aldan asked between chews. Cassidy nodded, knowing that he had reread her debriefing file before they left. "Then let's explore on our own and see what we can find."

Cassidy could hear his unspoken meaning. They would wait and see when it was at its most deserted before they attempted anything.

They wove their way toward the facility while Aldan ate. No one took notice of them as they walked, and Cassidy felt herself begin to relax. It wasn't much further to their destination. It wasn't much longer until she was able to go home....

The thought caused her to turn her attention to Aldan, and the unexpected sorrow she felt. She would be leaving him behind. He did say he wanted to see Earth, but...

The thought emptied out of her head, and she stopped in her tracks. There, ahead of them, was the same man who had been watching them outside the cafe. The one with the bright-orange hair.

Aldan took a step forward. His hard gaze was trained on the man in front of them. "Why have you been following us?"

Cassidy felt her eyebrows raise. Had Aldan noticed him tracking them this entire time?

The man reached into his pocket and pulled out a small black device. Cassidy opened her mouth to shout a warning, but it was too late. He pressed the large red button on the device before either of them could react.

Cassidy held her breath.

Nothing happened.

There was a click, and then a red light—the same

shade as the button under the man's thumb—began flashing on Aldan's gloves. Cassidy watched as his posture visibly relaxed.

The man stepped forward with a nod. "Aldan, I presume? I'm Nyler, your contracted tour guide. I've been waiting for you."

# CHAPTER ELEVEN

"I came early," Nyler said, leading them out of the public space and down a side alley. Buildings crowded around them, competing for space as they stretched up to the curved rock of the dome. The artificial sunlight was not as bright in the alley. "I wanted to make sure you weren't being followed before we connected."

Cassidy nodded. "Smart."

Nyler inclined his head, casting her a curious glance even as he led the way. "You are Cassidy Cane. The unexpected visitor who arrived on our planet last week." They were statements more than questions. When she nodded in response, he looked amused. "From the stories, I was picturing someone... taller."

Aldan covered a laugh with a cough and did his best to look innocent when she cast him a look.

"I can assure you that my short stature has no bearing on my capabilities," she replied, her tone indicating that she was speaking to both men.

A slow smile slid across Nyler's face. "Of that I have no doubt."

They fell silent as a group of school-aged children

passed them. Cassidy could see Aldan's expression as they passed, his eyes questioning as he watched the children as they hurried toward the courtyard together. Their skin looked ghastly pale in the dim lighting, a stark contrast to the colorful rock that surrounded them. They panted, struggling to fill their lungs with air at their quick pace. It was apparent that they were all several meals away from being considered underweight.

Aldan's expression was unreadable.

"What's the plan?" Cassidy asked Nyler once the children were out of earshot, hoping to distract Aldan out of whatever spiral his mind was taking and to restore his attention to the job at hand.

Nyler motioned up ahead. Cassidy could see the narrow alley widen again into a larger area, with several commercial buildings hugging the pathways. "A work crew is scheduled to arrive in the next few hours. They're on contract to conduct repairs to the air filtration system in the research facility."

"Big job," Aldan noted. Cassidy nodded in agreement, remembering the outside atmosphere and the lengths the citizens took to keep it outside of the safe zones.

"Big job, and an excellent opportunity to walk into the facility unnoticed."

Aldan frowned. "I assume we'll need credentials for that..."

"...which you will be providing?" Cassidy continued, noting that the end of the square had another seal to the outside planet, much like the one that they entered through. The difference was that this one seemed less inviting. No civilians milled around the barrier, and posted guards were checking ID bracelets of the people who were entering from the secure area.

Nyler nodded and led them to an adjacent building. The ease with which he navigated through the empty building had her breathing a sigh of relief.

"Here," he said, unlocking a small, windowless room and flicking on the lights so they could enter. When Aldan stared at him, refusing to move, Nyler rolled his eyes and stepped into the room first. "Fair enough," Cassidy heard him mutter.

She stepped into the room and looked around. It was a cross between a storage room and a locker room. Miscellaneous items were pushed against the wall—stacked chairs and broken benches—items so painfully boring that Cassidy was impressed by the ingenuity of the planet's small resistance faction. They hid well in plain sight.

Nyler unlocked one of the vertical cabinets and pulled out several hanging outfits for Aldan and Cassidy to try on. They reminded her of cloth coveralls from Earth, but instead of one large zipper to secure them, they automatically cinched to their bodies, folding in on themselves until they were secure around their waists, arms, and necks.

Cassidy pulled at the fabric around her neck, dismayed that it had less give than a turtleneck. "Is this really necessary?"

"Only if you want to get into the facility without detection. I can smell the atmosphere off of you from here. This should help to cover it. Besides," he nodded to Aldan, "your compound is about to wear off. I can see your skin tone breaking through."

He was right. The pigment cream that Aldan had used

had already started to decay from the chemicals of the atmosphere, and she could see patches of his red skin peeking through like rusty undertones. Cassidy sighed but said nothing. This was their show. A deal was a deal. She was so accustomed to working alone—sneaking into places after dark, or climbing into ancient sites to retrieve priceless artifacts—that the idea of waltzing into a restricted destination with a crowd of people during the day seemed completely foreign to her. More foreign than jumping through invisible portals onto alien worlds, somehow.

Nyler popped open a hidden drawer at the back of the locker. "I'll go check and see when the repair team arrives. We'll join them when they do." He tossed them each an ID bracelet before closing the locker. "Put these on. It's unlikely that everyone will be scanned again so soon after arrival, but you might as well look the part."

Aldan frowned and snapped the bracelet over his wrist. There was a humming sound, and it retracted into itself until it sat flush against his skin. A pale purple light began to blink along the top. "And if they do decide to scan everyone again?"

Nyler grinned. "Improvise."

# CHAPTER TWELVE

Cassidy resisted the urge to tug at her uniform. Instead, she kept her arms clamped to her sides as she marched with Aldan and Nyler and the rest of the repair crew into the large government building. Guards in brick-red uniforms stood posted at the entranceway, a precaution that had been implemented since Cassidy had last been there, scanning the crowd intermittently as the workers entered through the automated doors. She hastily scoured the area around her and was relieved that there were no familiar faces present.

Not that they would recognize her dressed like this. None of the work crew's faces were visible around their masks.

Last time Elona had led her through a small side-corridor. This time she entered through the front door. They marched into the foyer, the double doors hissed shut behind them with a finality that Cassidy felt in her spine. She would be glad when she could put this place behind her.

"Team A, you're to work on the 8th Floor," a voice boomed from the front of the room, causing everyone to become still. "Team B, Section 1: you're to go to the 11th Floor; Section 2: the basement." There was grumbling around them, but the director clapped their hands. "Move out, people. Those atmospheric leaks aren't going to fix themselves."

"C'mon," she motioned to Aldan and followed after Section 1. An elevator, much different from the secure, open-air one she had used last time, waited ahead of them. Cassidy waved her hand over the scanner and it answered with a musical chime as the elevator moved down to their floor. "Going up," she called out, inserting her hand into the door sensor after it arrived in order to keep it open. "11th Floor. After you. I insist."

Aldan watched her, wide-eyed, as she verbally herded Section 1 into the machine. "Squeeze in. There you go." Nyler gave her a nod from the elevator, and she removed her hand. The door slid closed with a warning bell. "You go ahead! We'll catch the next one. Yes, I insist. Thanks so much!"

Multiple pairs of eyes watched her with surprise between their safety masks as the door closed between them. Cassidy chuckled and turned to Aldan, who was also staring at her in surprise. "Lemmings."

Aldan looked perplexed. "What?"

"Never mind," she replied, remembering they were an Earth animal. She waited until the elevator was several floors up before running her hand through the scanner. An answering ding lit up the indicator, and a second elevator responded to her summons.

The door whooshed open, and they stepped inside. Aldan frowned at all the options. "I assume you know where you're going."

Cassidy pressed the button to the top floor without hesitation. "I have a very good memory."

"And if you're wrong?"

Cassidy gave a smirk, adjusting her hat and checking that her red hair stayed concealed. "Then we'll improvise."

Aldan muttered something under his breath that she couldn't quite make out, but from his tone she could tell that it wasn't flattering. She gave a soft laugh and he grinned in response.

A gentle chime announced their arrival and they sobered instantly. The door opened into a dark corridor, and Cassidy could feel Aldan shift his weight as he pressed a hand against his thigh. She knew he carried some sort of concealed weapon, but she had assumed it was in the pack that he'd refused to relinquish to Nyler in the storage room.

At least he came prepared.

The two stepped onto the floor, Cassidy mincing behind Aldan as he took the lead.

"According to our intel, there's a main computer that can access all the schematic databases." His voice was hushed in the dark hallway.

Cassidy knew which room he was talking about. "The war room," she confirmed. When he looked at her in surprise, she nodded ahead of them to the lone door in the corridor. The lift that she had taken last time on the other side of it. "I've been here already."

Aldan surveyed the locked door. He peered at the screen next to it, eyes narrowing as he tried to make sense of the shifting colors. "I wasn't expecting this type of lock-ing mechanism," he said at last.

"The code was a rainbow pattern," Cassidy offered, feeling unhelpful at best. Surprisingly, this seemed to mean something to him, and he keyed in a few different codes before it accepted one of them.

The door clicked open and swung inward.

"Paydirt," she told Aldan.

Aldan gave her a strange look, his expression clearly skeptical as he assessed her cognitive abilities. "It's not dirt, it's a growing agent. And we want the computer the information is stored on—"

Cassidy resisted the urge to sigh and stepped back. "Whatever it is, it's in there."

Aldan rolled his eyes and toed the door open further with his boot. The room was silent and dark, save for a few lights that flashed on one of the consoles that lined the walls. As they walked across the floor, large fluores-cent lights popped into existence above them. Cassidy led the way to a giant desk that commanded the room. She frowned at the dark surface of the desk. Without the lights, it looked like an ordinary meeting table.

"What…" she frowned and looked around its base for a hint of wires or plugs. "I swear this is it."

Aldan said nothing and scanned the room.

"Aren't you going to help?" She demanded, exasper-ated.

"Help poke at the giant machine that obviously isn't doing the one thing it's supposed to be doing in the only place it's supposed to be?" he drawled, ignoring the glare she shot at him as he continued to inspect the floor. His eyes ran along a perpendicular seam in the carpet that intersected with the corner of the desk. He smirked. "Sure."

Cassidy pressed her fists into her hips and watched as he made a show of walking along the carpet seam where it met the table. Finding nothing, he probed the raised fabric with a finger, then, to her surprise, peeled back that section of the carpet to uncover a coiled wire that connected to the table.

Making a noise of satisfaction in his throat, he tapped a dial on his glove and pressed a finger into the wire. An electrical jolt passed from his glove and sparked along the metal and into the table.

There was a click, then the sound of moving gears as a section of the tabletop moved and an internal compartment raised the large screen into view.

Cassidy stepped forward. "Clever."

Aldan reached around her and began waving a hand over the screen. His fingers activated unseen sensors, and Cassidy watched as Aldan navigated seamlessly through invisible settings to flip through various folders on the machine.

The muted chime of an arriving elevator broke the silence. Cassidy felt the back of her neck prickle and she turned her attention to the hallway. "Aldan," she warned.

Aldan looked up with a grimace. "I need more time."

Cassidy sucked in a quick breath while her mind raced. Giving a nod, she sprinted to the open door and closed it carefully, holding the thick metal door as best she could so that it closed with the barest click of the latch.

The locking mechanism clicked.

The lights dimmed in response, and Cassidy crouched down out of habit.

Aldan did the same, placing the desk between himself and the hallway, but continued sorting through the files to find what he was looking for.

There was the sound of approaching footsteps, and Cassidy held her breath as she heard the guards spread out along the hallway.

There was a rattling of the doorknob, but the door didn't budge.

"Check the alarm system," a gruff voice commanded. "I'm positive this was the office that was set off." The guard tried the door again to no avail.

Cassidy crept toward Aldan as the guards prowled toward the back elevator. He'd placed a small device on the monitor and was watching it as the light on it blinked at an intermittent tempo.

"Now would be a good time to go," she hissed.

"Not yet," he murmured, watching as the light sped up.

They both looked up as footsteps rushed down the hall.

"Now," Cassidy insisted.

Aldan flicked his eyes to the triangular device. The blinking light had become one solid color as the information transfer finished. "Let's go."

He snatched the transfer stick from the terminal just as the door swung open. "Not that way," he pivoted toward the back of the room.

Cassidy stared at him and the wall of windows behind them. "What…" but she had no time to finish her question. He grabbed her hand as he ran past, pulling her with him. "They don't open!" she protested, moving with him. This floor was high enough that it was above the confines of the dome. Cassidy guessed that they had found it easier to fortify this area of the building instead of raising the rocky barrier to its height.

Aldan secured his pack over his shoulders with his free hand, clipping the straps together across his chest. "Then we'll have to open them."

They stopped at the large windows. Aldan pulled a wire from his pack and secured it around the sturdy atmospheric pipes at the base of the window, then he pressed a thin disc to the glass—the same type of device he used for the door—turning it so that it stuck to the surface. He tapped it, and it began to emit a high-pitched whine. Cassidy backed up as thin cracks spread out of the disc like glistening spiderwebs.

The war room door was kicked open and the guards poured into the room.

"Let's go!" Aldan grabbed her hand and pulled her against him. His arms around her were strong as he held her tight against him. He turned so that their backs were to the glass. "Brace yourself!"

Before Cassidy could respond, Aldan launched them against the window with a powerful push of his legs. He grunted at the impact, but the glass remained intact.

Despite herself, a laugh bubbled out of Cassidy at the absurdity of the situation. She could feel Aldan's flaming cheek next to hers and she began to laugh in earnest.

"Very funny," he muttered.

Cassidy didn't know if it was her lack of sleep that

was driving her reaction, or his embarrassment at the failed escape attempt, but another laugh escaped her lips. "S-sorry."

Aldan huffed and peered over her shoulder at his gloves. He tapped the activator button and the disc behind them caused the glass to pop. "I was distracted," he muttered, pulling her close.

Cassidy felt her heartbeat speed up.

The guards took their positions. "Stop right there!" The commander ordered. "You're under arrest!"

"Only if you catch us." Aldan taunted, launching them against the window.

This time the glass broke on contact.

A breathless scream escaped Cassidy's lips as they plummeted through the open air. Panic gripped her mind until the sound of the extending metal cord filled her ears. She willed herself to calm down even as her fingers bit into Aldan's arm in a death-grip.

Spelunking. They were just spelunking.

Large shards of glass from the window clinked harmlessly off of her face mask. The smaller pieces had been sucked into the room from the force of the vacuum that Aldan had created. Whether it had been strategic or not she didn't know, but it had done the trick. The guards' screams followed them as they fell. The horror apparent in their tone as the noxious atmosphere rushed into the room where they stood.

At least they were too busy to attempt to break their metal lifeline.

Cassidy shut out the sound of their voices. Instead, she concentrated on the rocky top of the atmospheric dome as they plummeted toward it.

They were falling at an incredible speed.

Aldan's arms were locked tight around her. Cassidy craned her neck around and called his name, but he ignored her. Instead of watching the spooling metal line, or the quickly-approaching rocky red surface, his eyes were glued to the passing windows. She watched as his eyes darted from one window to the next, his gaze hurriedly flicked over the panes of glass as they fell.

What was he looking for?

Cassidy's heart pounded. She faced forward and scanned the windows. The outline of their falling form was reflected back at her in the glass. The light was bright enough that she could barely see into the rooms if she adjusted her focus, but nothing of any consequence stood out at her. No glaringly-obvious sign of what Aldan was looking for.

Except…

She jerked her head to the side. The relentless sun sliced into a fractured spiderweb. There, sitting in the middle of the stretching faucets, was a thin metal disc. A suggestion of a shadow that hung as a sign of their salvation.

"There!" Cassidy pointed with a scream.

Aldan's reaction was immediate. He clenched a fist and the metal wire snapped with the tension of their weight. He grunted in her ear, arms locked around her as the give in the rope disappeared, his pack acting like a harness similar to the ones they had used to scale down the cliffs earlier.

Cassidy had twined her legs around his, determined that there was no way she would allow him to drop her.

She didn't have to worry. The abrupt halt in their descent caused them to swing toward the building. Aldan lifted his legs—and Cassidy's—in front of them and angled his feet so that the heels of his boots made the first impact. They hit their mark, slamming into the metal disc with the full force of their combined weights, causing the fractured window to shatter around them as they were thrown into the room.

At some point they became untangled from each other. Cassidy flew ahead of him into the room. She caught herself by rolling across the plush carpet to spread out the impact of her landing. Her mask, the side strap sliced through from the jagged window, flew off of her face with the movement. She came to a halt on her back, splayed only a few feet away from where Aldan was groaning. The tingling in her fingers had nothing to do with how tightly she had gripped the straps around his chest. She propped herself up on an elbow to assess him, grinning when he groaned again, then flopped back over to catch her breath.

With her head cushioned against the floor, and nothing but the sound of their labored breathing filling the room, Cassidy couldn't help herself as the absurdity of the situation caught up with her.

She laughed.

There was an edge of tension to it that she didn't quite feel, as if her own hysteria was hiding from her somehow. The sound of it set her off even more, and before she knew it, tears were streaming down her face as laughter peeled out of her

She tried to control herself, only to realize that Aldan

had joined in and was laughing right along with her. Or maybe it was at her. She couldn't tell, and she certainly didn't care.

A helmeted head appeared over her and Nyler looked down at Cassidy with raised eyebrows. "Having fun?" he asked the two of them.

Cassidy's only response was a hiccup, and the sound was enough to push Aldan into another fit of laughter that had Nyler shaking his head in disbelief.

# CHAPTER THIRTEEN

Nyler helped Aldan and Cassidy to their feet. Cassidy could see the smirk that had settled on his face through the window in his mask. His dark eyes appraised them, focusing on the pack that Aldan had secured over his chest. An eyebrow raised in surprise, but he said nothing, and Cassidy could see that he understood why Aldan had refused to leave his pack at the storage locker.

There was a heartbeat of silence, and Nyler's eyes widened. His gaze darted between Cassidy and the broken window, and the obvious noxious atmosphere funneling into the room with a force that was strong enough to cause her hair to shift with the movement.

Nyler's expression was filled with awe. "So it is true," he breathed.

Cassidy realized that he wasn't staring at her hair color but at her face. At the space where her mask used to rest, and the ease of her breath without it.

He flicked his attention to Aldan, who had come to stand beside her like a supportive shadow. "I had heard the rumors but didn't believe... She can breathe the atmosphere..." When Aldan nodded, Nyler's expression shifted from shock to surprise. "As can you."

Aldan shifted a shoulder in a half-shrug. "Mostly," he conceded. His breath came easier than before, and Cassidy assumed the face mask blocked some of the chemicals that were swirling around them—a small measure of what Nyler's breathing mask could do.

"How?" the Alluvian demanded.

"His body has adapted," Cassidy replied, with a gentleness that she hoped matched the edge in Nyler's voice. "Tellurians function in their atmosphere without assistance. Their physiological changes mean increased lung strength and size for survival on their moon—something that helps on your planet."

The desperation on Nyler's face was apparent even with his breathing mask. "Could that happen for us as well?"

"Eventually..." Aldan stepped forward at the crack of emotion in the other man's voice. "That is our hope." His voice was low. "We want future generations to work together instead of against one another, so that they can create a life that benefits and heals both our peoples. But to accomplish this we will need the continued support of the Alluvian Resistance. We can't do it alone."

Cassidy stared at Aldan after his heart-felt speech, barely recognizing him without the swagger that seemed to be his default setting. She felt a knot loosen in her stomach, and for the first time since her initial arrival through the portal, she didn't feel stupid for being tricked by the Alluvians. Maybe it was something that needed to happen. Maybe it was the catalyst for their peoples finally working together.

Nyler stepped forward and extended a hand, clasping Aldan's forearm. "Then help you shall have."

A grin broke across Aldan's face. Usually, his expressions were filled with self-assured arrogance, but this one was colored with such relief and joy that Cassidy couldn't help but smile in response.

The relief was short-lived. Emergency lights flashed and a grating whine cut through the air. It was all Cassidy could do to keep from clapping her hands over her ears.

"Starting now," Nyler continued, as though the building hadn't burst into high alert. "That isn't related to the atmospheric leaks. Let's get you and that precious technology back to Telluria."

"Fantastic." Aldan glanced behind them at the smashed window, then at the interior of the building where the alarm continued its shrill warning. "How, exactly?"

Nyler frowned but Cassidy stepped forward. "Through the front door." When both men turned to her, brows raised with expectation, she flashed them a grin. "I have a plan, and I think it's going to be a lot of fun."

Nyler looked hopeful, but Aldan took one look at the glint in her eye and groaned.

\*\*\*

"I thought you said this was going to be fun," Aldan hissed at her, adjusting his position so that the barrel of the blaster was no longer digging into his spine.

"I meant for me," Cassidy clarified, nudging him forward with the weapon.

Aldan and Nyler held their hands high in surrender, marching before her toward the sterile-looking foyer.

Cassidy had discarded her worker's uniform in favour of her usual clothing and Aldan's pack, the only addition to her regular outfit. She had even unbound her hair, letting the snarls of curls—unkempt from days of adventuring—flow past her shoulders, flaunting her identity.

She didn't want any doubt who was terrorizing the Alluvian facility. And with any luck, Aldan and Nyler would appear as nothing but two faceless hostages.

She could hear the sound of people running toward them. She kept their pace unhurried, strutting across the massive stone lobby, maneuvering around the piles of dust and debris that were the result of the different explosions.

Security guards burst into the foyer. They lined off along the walls, shouting at the three as they trained their weapons on them.

Cassidy ignored them and kept moving.

"Don't shoot! Don't shoot!" Nyler and Aldan screamed, waving their hands in a show of desperation.

"Stop now or we'll open fire," roared an officer, stepping forward.

Cassidy's pulse quickened at the sound of her voice. The female officer had put herself between them and the door, but even from this distance, Cassidy recognized the strands of vibrant fuchsia hair that had escaped from the officer's black cap.

Elona.

Cassidy had considered the woman a friend of sorts when she first arrived. That was before the plan for her to sabotage the Tellurian crop had been formed. Before she discovered that Elona had been part of the deception that had sent Cassidy into certain death.

Elona's face had the same smooth, unreadable expression that it held when they first met. The only difference was that her pale purple eyes now pleaded with her to stop. She had never wanted to harm Cassidy. She had been following orders.

Cassidy slowed enough to show that she'd heard the command. Enough so that the others in front of her stopped moving. She had no intention of surrendering. If the Alluvians had planned to kill her for helping them, she didn't want to know what they would do to her for breaking their laws.

The thought strengthened her resolve. The area was silent. Cassidy made a show of lifting her hand and tapping her chest. "I wouldn't do that if I were you," she cautioned.

She felt the room's attention shift to where she tapped. Cassidy partially unzipped her coat and peeled back the outer layer. The room immediately felt tense as she displayed the clay explosives strapped to her chest.

A shove of her blaster into Nyler and Aldan's backs had them doing the same and they showed off their matching devices.

"Shoot any of us and this entire building blows." Cassidy's voice rang easily in the silence.

Elona's eyes widened. She raised a fist to the unit around them in a command to hold their positions. Then, after a long, assessing look at Cassidy, she begrudgingly stepped out of the way.

Cassidy inclined her head and nudged her hostages forward. She raised her other hand to show off the remote

detonator she held, her thumb hovering against the trig-
gering button. "Don't even think about shooting me in the
back!"

Elona cursed behind her as they exited the building...

...And came face-to-face with a squadron of soldiers.

Aldan and Nyler swore under their breath. Cassidy
was unable to join them as the sight of the brick-red wall
of uniformed military personnel surrounding them had
caused her mouth to go dry.

Large armored vehicles blocked their path. Unlike the
automated one that she had used for transit outside of the
dome, these ones were not air-tight, and clearly meant for
driving on the smooth paved streets. They spread out in
a u-shape, the apex of which sat opposite the doors of the
building they had just exited. Countless soldiers stood
in position between them, and Cassidy scanned the surrounding area for any activity.

Her steps faltered when she noted the snipers in position in the adjacent buildings. Her brain immediately
conjured possible scenarios as to how this standoff would
end—none of them in her favour—but she kept her gaze
focused on the men in front of her and the road ahead of
them.

"You better know what you're doing," Nyler mum-
bled, the slight tremble in his raised hands the only sign
of his nervousness.

"Trust us," Aldan whispered back, though Cassidy
could hear a twinge of uncertainty in his voice that she
hoped Nyler couldn't detect.

"We stick to the plan," she murmured, hoping her

voice projected a confidence that she didn't feel.

The crackle of a radio signal caught her attention. She met the dead-eyed stare of the blue-haired Captain Kruz as he lifted his head away from the communicator at his shoulder. His eyes flicked between the detonation device and the explosives they wore on their chests, and his lip curled in disgust as he took a step back.

*Good*, Cassidy thought. She felt a twinge of guilt at the expression on his face. She had met him previously while here—as well as his wife and young daughter—and she knew he was thinking of the threat she represented to his family.

Cassidy took a moment before steeling her spine. It didn't matter how he felt so long as he gave them their space.

"Lead the way," she commanded Nyler, her voice harsh. He marched them down the road and between the armoured vehicles, between the soldiers and the weapons they had trained on their bodies.

Cassidy made sure to keep the detonation device in full view.

Nyler unerringly led them to the square where they'd first entered the dome.

"It's empty," Aldan noted, his voice soft as he scanned the area.

Cassidy attempted to swallow past the dryness in her mouth. He was right. The area that had initially been so full of life when they arrived was now silent and deserted. The authorities had evacuated everyone once the alarm was activated, and that was either very good or very bad news for Cassidy.

"I don't like the look of this," Nyler muttered, confirming Cassidy's fear. "They're planning something."

"So are we," Cassidy countered with false bravado. She couldn't argue. There was no reason to evacuate such a large area next to the exit unless they were up to something.

Cassidy could hear the armoured vehicles following at a distance. She spared a glance behind her and was greeted by the sight of the entire squadron inching along after them.

"We've got company," Aldan warned.

Cassidy jerked her attention forward and watched as another squadron of soldiers blocked off the entries to the side streets. With their weapons cocked, she couldn't help but feel as though they were herding them toward the exit.

Aldan twisted his head to the side, his eyes narrowing when he caught sight of the armed gauntlet. "Not good."

"We don't have much of a choice," Cassidy replied through gritted teeth.

"Maybe you don't," Nyler murmured, "but I do."

Before she could respond, the Alluvian began to scream. Everyone jerked to attention at the sound, then tensed as Nyler ran—still screaming—away from Cassidy and toward the nearest armoured car.

Cassidy stared after him, dumbfounded.

"Grab me," Aldan hissed at her.

"What?"

"You're the Tellurian Terrorist—act like it. *Grab me.*"

That was all she needed. Cassidy grabbed Aldan's hand and twisted his arm behind his back.

The maneuver was awkward. Aldan had a foot on her height and almost twice as much muscle mass over her. She was forced to look around him as looking over his shoulder wasn't an option.

"Convincing," he grunted, trying to wiggle his arm loose to provide some relief, but Cassidy's grip on his arm didn't allow it.

Resting the blaster against his head she marched them forward. All eyes followed them, and she could feel the squadron's attention centre on her hand that now held both the weapon and the detonator.

"They're going to shoot us. You know that, right?"

"The thought had crossed my mind."

"And?"

"And I'm open to suggestions."

Aldan remained quiet, his silence pensive.

"Okay, let's run through it," Cassidy said in her best lecturer's voice. "If we leave the dome, they shoot us because they're no longer at risk of getting blown up."

"And we still are."

"Precisely."

"All right. So, we'll need a method of escape once we're out there."

"Any suggestions on how to accomplish that?"

"Definitely not."

"Great." Cassidy eyed the approaching barrier.

"Stalling won't work." When Cassidy didn't answer, Aldan continued. "They'll call our bluff about detonating and capture us."

Cassidy hummed in agreement. She wracked her brain trying to think of an alternative plan.

A commotion behind them interrupted her train of thought. There was the sound of yelling, and Cassidy turned to witness a scuffle where Nyler had joined their ranks.

Aldan stopped short. "What the—"

An engine revved. The sound seemed thunderous in the tense silence that surrounded the stalemate. Soldiers scrambled to break formation as an armoured vehicle lurched into the square and slammed on the acceleration.

The sound of blaster fire rang out and the pair ducked.

"Hold your fire!" the commander screamed. "You'll blow the dome!"

The vehicle barrelled toward Cassidy and Aldan without showing signs of slowing. Cassidy had readied herself to launch out of the way when Aldan wrapped an arm around her waist. "Wrong way."

"What!"

"Hold on!"

Before she could protest, he stepped into the path of the oncoming vehicle. Cassidy unceremoniously jammed the detonation device into her pocket—the silly thing hadn't been activated to begin with—and squeezed her eyes shut.

The armoured truck swerved, and Aldan grabbed one of the railings that wrapped around the side of it. Grunting, he swung them up into the bed of the truck.

"Glad you could make it," Nyler quipped through the back opening of the cab from where he sat in the driver's seat.

"Took you long enough," Aldan shot back.

Nyler grinned in response and slammed the driving gear to its fastest setting. They sped toward the barrier. "I wanted to give you time to come up with a plan."

"You should've taken longer, then." Aldan looked down and realized his arm was still around Cassidy's waist. His face reddened around the mask he wore. He opened his mouth to say something, then jerked his head back toward the square. "Duck!"

Cassidy dropped to her knees as a beam of light shot past them in a wide arc. The ground rumbled where it made contact.

"That wasn't even close," Nyler shouted back at them. "It's like they were trying to miss."

"They are." Cassidy shaded her eyes with a hand and assessed the soldiers behind them.

Aldan's expression was one of grim agreement. "They're herding us."

"To where?"

"To where they can detonate us safely."

Cassidy heard Nyler's sharp intake of breath. "Why?" The question was desperate.

Aldan's gaze flicked to where the transfer device was hidden in his inside pocket.

"Because they never had any intention of letting us escape." Cassidy frowned. "They've been waiting for the best moment to get rid of us with the least amount of damage."

Nyler's driving didn't falter. "So what do we do?"

Cassidy pursed her lips. She slid her gaze from the pocket inside Aldan's open coat, to the explosive device that was still wrapped around his chest. She looked at the one strapped around her own torso, then raised her eyes to Aldan's. "We give them what they want."

"What?"

"They want an explosion? Let's give them one." Cassidy banged her hand on the top of the driver's cab. "Slow down, Nyler."

Nyler looked at her with surprise but did as he was told.

Aldan looked thoughtful as Cassidy climbed between them, unclasping their explosive devices and holding them by the straps. She waited until they approached the barrier.

"I hope you didn't get kicked out of the military for being a lousy shot," she said to Aldan as she began to swing one of the devices in a circular motion, using the strap as a sling.

Aldan ripped his mask off and grinned, sliding his blaster from his belt holster just as Cassidy lobbed the first brick of clay into the air. She waited several heartbeats before releasing the next one, and then the next, timing it so that they synced into the same, spaced-out, downward arch.

Aldan cocked his weapon. "Go," he told Nyler, who slammed the vehicle into top speed.

He fired one shot and the device closest to them exploded. The resulting force bridged the gap and set off the other explosives, rocking the area around them.

Cassidy was thrown backward from the force. She slammed into the cab of the vehicle and grabbed the side to keep from falling off. Next to her Aldan did the same. The back tires lifted off the road before smashing back down with an impact that jarred her bones.

Surprise and horror sent a chill down her spine as they sped through the exit and away from the dome.

The explosions had caught the dome's slanted ceiling. The inside shield wasn't as strong as the outside by design. The outside rock was fortified against the atmospheric chemicals, and a huge section had blown outward from the force, creating a gaping hole that now acted as a vacuum.

The soldiers were too preoccupied to follow them as the trio sped into the wasteland. Alarm bells rang and lights flashed. Cassidy stared wide-eyed at the commotion behind them as the mobilized forces fell back to safer ground. She could see them moving their equipment to erect a barricade under the crumbling rock.

Next to her, Aldan lowered his blaster in surprise. "Oops."

# CHAPTER FOURTEEN

Cassidy kept her gaze focused on the approaching mountain range ahead of them.

Aldan holstered his blaster and stood next to her. "No one got hurt, Cassidy." His voice was gentle as he answered her unasked question.

Cassidy couldn't meet his eye. "How do you know?"

Aldan shrugged a shoulder. "The military provides blast-resistance uniforms. And the block had already been evacuated—there were no civilians to injure."

Cassidy eyed his coat and remembered how it had snapped into a shield to protect them. She frowned. "But the atmosphere—"

"—Is inconsequential." Aldan gave her a lopsided grin. "The domes can fail at any moment. Every building has masks and an evaluation plan in place for that possibility."

Cassidy felt the tension from her shoulders disappear. There was no reason for him to lie. He'd been nothing but honest with her up until this point.

Aldan took a step closer, and Cassidy found herself looking up into his yellow eyes. "You have a fierce and beautiful heart, Cassidy Cane."

Cassidy felt her cheeks heat at his words.

"We've got company," Nyler warned. His voice was muffled by the breathing mask he slapped on when they exited the dome.

Aldan and Cassidy turned. One of the army vehicles had broken away from the barricade to pursue them through the wasteland.

Aldan swore.

A shadow fell across them as Nyler entered the mountain range.

"Pull in over there," Aldan told Nyler, pointing to a large hollow ahead in the distance. "We'll have to double back to throw them off our trail."

"We?"

"Aren't you coming with us?" Aldan cocked his head at Nyler. "Unless you'd rather wait here for the soldiers to arrive…"

Nyler grinned. "I thought you'd never ask." He expertly maneuvered the stolen vehicle under the rocky overhang before killing the engine. The three of them hopped down and began to pile loose stones and boulders along the side to partially cover it.

Cassidy surveyed their handiwork. It looked like a botched hiding attempt. Their pursuers would be drawn to it immediately. It was perfect. "Let's go."

Aldan led the way to the cave where he and Cassidy had appeared earlier that day.

Nyler gave them an incredulous look when they entered. "What are you doing?"

Cassidy fought the urge to grin. She couldn't blame

his hesitation. It looked as though they were dragging him into an underground tunnel.

Well, they were. But this one had a hidden exit.

She stepped into the tunnel, motioning for Nyler to follow her. Her arms were outstretched as she walked, using them to feel the edges of the tunnel as they hurried through it and into the cave at the end. Almost immediately, she could feel the familiar prickle of a nearby portal on her right. Moving closer, she plunged her hand into it without hesitation, feeling the shock of cold that reverberated down her arm just as Aldan illuminated it with his gloves.

Nyler's jaw dropped when he saw her arm disappear into the solid rock wall. "How…?"

Cassidy didn't answer. Instead, she pulled her arm back out. She kept her left hand against the cave wall and took a few steps forward. There, ahead in the distance, she could feel the faint pull of a second portal.

It was the portal home.

"It's a secret." Aldan's tone was light, but his expression said it all—it was a secret to be protected. He stepped toward her and motioned for Cassidy to turn around, rummaging in the pack she still wore to pull out several force shield projectors.

He took a moment to assess where to place them, finally choosing spots where, once the wall was formed, it would offer no view of the cave past the tunnel.

"I can't block the whole tunnel. They would notice that. But this cave should suffice." Aldan brought the projectors online with a few taps of his glove.

With a start, Cassidy realized that, unlike on Telluria,

Aldan wasn't creating a barrier to the cave, he was going to fill in the entire cave. He wasn't taking any chances of the Alluvians breaking through an unmonitored rock wall and finding the way to Telluria.

"I hope your device works quickly," Nyler frowned.

Aldan winced in agreement. "The visual projection powers up first, then the force shield. So long as they don't stick their arms in it…" He walked around the cave, attaching more of the projectors to the walls as he did. With a single tap against his glove, he activated them. "That should do it."

The two men looked expectantly at Cassidy.

"Is it safe?" she asked.

Aldan gave a gentle smile, knowing what she meant. "Our reinforcements would have arrived long before now to cause a distraction. If there had been a problem, the Tellurian government would have come through the portal as soon as they discovered it.

Cassidy nodded. That made sense. There was no danger in them returning to Telluria.

Aldan inclined his head. "Shall we?"

"No."

The word came out more hollow than she intended.

Nyler's eyes widened, but Cassidy barely noticed as her attention was mostly focused on Aldan. His stare burned into her as she took a step sideways—not forward—around the Tellurian portal.

She could feel the pull of the second portal. The one that she had missed the last time she returned from Alluvia. The one that led to Earth. "I have to go home."

The only sound was the rock wall building itself along

the parameters Aldan had programmed. He stepped forward and extended a hand. Not for her, she realized, but for the pack she still wore across her back. Aldan flipped it open then, to her surprise, simply closed it again and returned it to her. She slung it slowly over one shoulder.

"Cassidy…" Aldan's expression was unreadable. There was a beat of silence, then he and Nyler snapped to attention—their keen sense of hearing picking up what Cassidy's could not. "Go."

"They're coming," Nyler declared at the same instant. In his haste, he stepped backwards into the tunnel that led to Telluria. Caddisy could see his expression of surprise before he disappeared completely into the rock face.

Aldan's eyes flicked to the wall that was slowly building itself into the empty space of the tunnel, then back to her as she stood there, halfway between the two portals.

Their eyes met for the briefest of moments. "*Go,*" he said again, his voice soft.

She could hear the approaching soldiers. The wall projection blocked them from view, but Cassidy knew that the shield was not yet fully functional, and she fervently hoped that they wouldn't think to inspect the back wall of the tunnel.

Aldan grasped Cassidy's arms and turned her so that she was facing him. He gave her a smile, a smile that lit up his yellow eyes and caused her fingertips to tingle, then pushed her backward without warning.

He watched her as she fell, his expression unreadable.

He gave her one last look, then pivoted and threw himself after Nyler as the cave closed in on itself. He disappeared as Alluvia faded from sight, and the view of the planet became obstructed by a solid rock wall that had appeared from thin air.

***

Cassidy slammed into the ground, catching herself with her elbow to lessen the impact. She lay there for several minutes, breathing, as she waited and reoriented herself.

She was alone.

The air was unmistakably familiar. She took gasping breaths, feeling relief as the noxious vapors from Alluvia were expelled from her lungs and replaced with the sweet-smelling air from her home planet.

She was back on Earth.

Cassidy groaned and sat up, carefully sliding Aldan's pack to the ground. Opening the top flap, she spied the object that Aldan had placed in there—a folded over piece of fabric. She pulled it open and was surprised to see alien, hand-written lettering had been burned into it—undoubtedly another function of the multi-purpose gloves that he wore. She held it up to get a better look.

> *Use these crumbs to find your way back.*
> *Your Hansel,*
> *Aldan.*

Cassidy peered inside the pack and was amazed at the Tellurian technology that Aldan had allowed her to bring back to Earth. She tucked the note into her coat pocket and secured the pack. Gamgee would be delighted to get his hands on these inventions, but there was no real scientific reason for her to turn over the note. Besides, he would probably hear all about it soon enough.

Cassidy rose and dusted off her pants, turning in the direction where she had left her car all those days ago.

A large grin spread across her face as she began to make her way home. Cassidy had a feeling that this wouldn't be the last of the Tellurian Terrorist.

# EPILOGUE

Tallis stood alone in the park, squeezing his stress ball in his hand. He was standing beside the see-saw where there were children playing, but he was not with them nor was he watching them.

In the far distance, far enough away that they wouldn't have noticed him staring even if they'd looked in his direction, a family of four walked together along the foot path.

It was Preston and Kayla Cane and two of their three children, Margo and Rica. They walked and laughed and ate ice cream and talked about something pleasant he couldn't make out.

As he watched them, he started to squeeze the stress ball harder, and faster.

# THE COMING OF TALLIS

## MATTHEW LEDREW & JD RYOT

# CHAPTER ONE

Cassidy Cane ran from the laser fire with a big smile on her face, even though some of it was close enough to pass through her jacket and make sizzling holes in it. Despite the danger, her blood was pumping. In her hand she had clasped the Amulet of Zeus, one of the ten fabled Amulets of the Ok'Tid. Only one still existed on her world, with the rest lost to history, but on this world the population had found a way to perfectly preserve artifacts.

She had been looking for a way to copy that technology for use on her adventures, both at home and on other worlds, but then she had seen the Amulet and something about it had called to her and she had just had to touch it. She had felt that blood pumping in her ears and the smile had grown on her cheeks and she had just needed to have her hand against it. It looked so new here, not like the one she'd seen back home.

The moment her skin had connected with it alarms had started to go off, and all the faces in the museum she'd been visiting turned and glared at her as one, as though they were a hive mind.

"I guess that's the end of that," she'd said. Her voice was resigned but she had not been able to quell the smile growing across her lips. She had gripped her hand around the artifact almost instinctively, and when she had turned to run, she ran with it.

As she watched, the people of this dimension turned their heads and followed her, then quickly transformed into cat people. Their noses and mouths came together in snouts and they grew hair quickly, as though it had been waiting under the skin for the chance to emerge all this time. They hissed, raised their laser weapons, and started after her.

They fired at her again, and she felt a hot beam whiz past her neck so close that it tanned it. Despite the fear she should have been feeling, the blood was pumping in her so hard that she could feel it in her earlobes and in her fingers, and she smiled broadly and honestly.

She rounded a corner into a corridor that seemed to have no exit and started down it quickly.

The cat people turned around the same corner less than thirty seconds later in hot pursuit, but they found it empty. There was no trace of Cassidy Cane, or the Amulet of Zeus. The lead guard lowered its brow, curled its lip, and hissed. "Slipstreamer."

\*\*\*

Preston Cane sat on the park bench alone. Even though there were no people with him – not his wife or any of his daughters – he didn't feel alone. He had his bag of bird-seed with him, and pigeons had flocked to his feet to take his gift. Some days, when the sun was hot and the breeze was good, they were all the company he needed.

"Hello," said a man with black hair and a slender face. He sat down on the bench next to Preston and set a sack lunch between them. "Mind if I join you?"

Preston turned and looked at him, shocked out of his train of thought for a moment. "Absolutely not; to each their own."

The man nodded, then reached into his bag and pulled out two halves of a sandwich. He handed one to Preston. "Cucumber sandwich?"

Preston eyed it hungrily. "That's my favourite."

"Take it, then."

Preston took the half gratefully, and both men started eating. "I'm Preston, by the way," he said, extending his free hand.

The man took it. "Tallis."

# CHAPTER TWO

The Plainsfield Mall was one of those standard two-floor mall layouts that seemed to come standard with every town in America of over 50,000 residents. It was long and flat and took up far too much acreage for the benefits it provided. Despite how large it was, most of the space was taken up by wide halls: except the top floor, which had ninety percent of its middle carved out so that pedestrians could look down and see the patrons and storefronts below.

Cassidy stepped past a trendy outwear shop towards the food court in the heart of the building, bypassing adults and children as she did. She eyed a bomber jacket on a window-displayed mannequin that looked startlingly like the one she wore, but without the barrage of holes, and considered it. Seeing it in its 'complete' state made her suddenly aware of the state that her own had gotten into over the course of the last year. There were tears from getting caught in the thorns of plants on other worlds. There were bullet holes from fire she'd barely evaded. There were places where the fabric had gone rough from going from extreme hot to extreme cold too quickly, between portals. She wore the history of her adventures along her shoulders, she realized, and though the new coat made her realize how ripped and torn her current one was, she smiled and wore those tears with pride.

She eyed the jacket just once more, then continued on deeper into the mall. It was filled with people today, and she could already see the glut of them sitting at the food court. There were so many that she couldn't tell one from the other. She knew that Rica was amongst them somewhere though, and from the last text she'd gotten, she'd already nabbed a clean seat and was waiting for her.

Frederica was nineteen and in all those years she had never once been called by her full name by someone close enough to have known her, as far as Cassidy could remember. She had always been Rica. Whenever her full name, Frederica, had been said over the loudspeaker at school it had always taken her a moment to realize they were talking to her. It was a name that sounded foreign to her ear, despite being technically hers. Of Cassidy's two sisters, Rica was the quieter of the two. She hadn't graduated yet, but was planning on attending Plainsfield University when she did, and had politely asked Cassidy not to put herself into the process, one way or the other. Cassidy had respected that. Soon it would be that time, and Cassidy was anxious to see the result.

Months ago, while she was on a space station in the Xik'en dimension, she'd met a bright young woman who had reminded her so much of Rica, and had vowed to herself to make more time for her family in general and her sisters in specific. She had managed to make more time for them in the months that had followed, even despite her time off-world. As soon as she'd arrived back on her own Earth, she had made a point of making a date with Rica.

Cassidy smiled as she entered the food court proper. Nothing smelled quite like familiarity. It was something she'd learned on her travels to other parts of this world as well as to other worlds: nothing smelled quite like the food of home. The food court was full of local restaurants producing fresh bread, baking pizzas, slicing sandwiches, and brewing fresh coffee. There were several large chains as well, but they couldn't compete for her business or for her olfactory sensations.

She turned, near the edge of the seating area now, and tried to find where Rica had been seated. Was she still lined up for food? A quick scan of those standing told her no.

A large group of tweens stood up at once and started to walk towards the exit, clearly a group of school-age kids that were nearing the end of their lunch break. She wondered how many of them she'd be seeing in her classroom in the next few years. They dispersed, and as they parted she finally caught sight of Rica, seated on the far end of the food court away from her. Her back had been turned to Cassidy, the barest sliver of her round cheek visible.

She was talking to a man.

He was older than Rica by far, closer to Cassidy's age if not actually her age. He was broad and had dark black hair that fell into his eyes the way a pop-singer's did in all their promotional photos. He was wearing a tight black shirt that accented his frame and made him look even paler than he naturally was, and jeans. He had one boot up on the chair across from Rica and had the weight of his arms leaning against his knee. His boots were the thick-soled kind like her own, the sort that were gotten from army surplus outlets. His were black.

Despite his aggressive posture, looming over the sitting Rica, he was smiling warmly. He was laughing at something she'd said, and in that moment Cassidy could not tell if the laugh was fake or genuine.

Cassidy squinted. She could tell from the push of her sister's cheek that she was smiling. She started to make her way past the crowd and through the winding grid of tables to get to them.

The man in black looked up and locked eyes with her, and she stopped dead in her tracks for a moment. There was something uncanny about him staring at her that caused her to pause. They were pinned between each other like that, and time around them seemed to stop.

Then he broke the spell, suddenly, by turning back to Rica and nodding a goodbye before turning his back on her completely and walking away from the food court.

"Hey, wait!" Cassidy called. She found her legs again and started to weave her way through the tables and over chairs to catch him.

Rica turned around at the sound of her sister's voice. "Cassidy?"

The man in black stepped away from the court and down a long hallway that Cassidy knew led only to a maintenance area. There was no escape that way, and she found herself grinning, though she wasn't sure why.

She stepped past Rica, whose gaze turned to follow

her.

"Cassidy, what are you doing?"

Cassidy turned the sharp corner leading down the long hallway to the maintenance area and found... nothing. Just a long, empty hallway with no doors or windows until the very end. She paused, her smile fading and that familiar uptick of her pulse that got her blood moving subsiding. She stood in the mouth of the hall for a moment, as if expecting the stark white walls to produce his black-clad from thin air. She let out a long sigh.

"What is wrong with you?" Rica said, laughing as she met her sister and followed her gaze down the corridor.

"Who was that guy?" Cassidy asked, her tone more serious than even she had expected it to be. She swallowed, controlling herself.

"Just some guy. He said he liked my bag while he was waiting in line at the taco stand."

"Was he hitting on you?"

"What? Ugh. No," Rica warbled. She thought about it for a moment, the idea planted in her head now, then shook it away again. "No, it wasn't like that. He was sweet."

"A lot of older guys pretend to be sweet."

"It was... avuncular," Rica said, finding the word with the same gusto with which Cassidy found artifacts.

Cassidy turned to her, eyebrow raised. "That's a word."

Rica grinned. "There wasn't anything going on, I swear. People can just talk to me, you know."

Cassidy's mouth warbled, and she realized that she was not winning this argument. Reluctantly, she agreed to put it to bed, and they went back to the food court to get a meal of Yackko's Tacos, on Cassidy. They enjoyed the rest of their meal, talking about school and university and summer jobs, and before long the normalcy of it all eroded away the strangeness of the way the exchange had begun.

Without either of them seeing, the man in black named Tallis stepped out of the long hallway, found them with his gaze, then turned and left the mall.

# CHAPTER THREE

Every time she stepped into Gamgee's lab, Cassidy felt a sense of wonder.

She hadn't the first time, all those months ago, because she hadn't known exactly what the lab had represented. The first time she'd entered, on Gamgee's invitation, it hadn't felt like taking the first steps into the lab were also taking the first steps into adventure. Now she knew it was, and that knowledge in the back of her head always brought with it a certain tingle of anticipation: what would happen next?

This time, that feeling turned to ash in her mouth as her eyes adjusted to the light from outside and revealed the lab to be torn apart. The smile faded from her face as her eyes found Gamgee, fighting with a fire extinguisher to put out a blaze happening inside his control panel. The extinguisher sputtered, and he cursed a word she'd never heard him say before.

"Gamgee!" she exclaimed, crossing the room in great running leaps. She took the extinguisher from him, primed it, then braced its base between her legs and took aim at the base of the flame with the nozzle. She fired a steady stream of white foam that doused it totally, ending the threat, then let the extinguisher fall to the floor.

She huffed, both their breaths laboured as they took in lungfuls of burning, plasticy air. She turned around the lab slowly now that the immediate danger was done, allowing herself to take in the totality of the destruction. Her first thought when she'd seen it all was that it had been an explosion – that Gamgee had been testing some fantastical device she'd brought back from another world, only to have had it blow up in his face. Now that the danger was less clear and present, she saw immediately that that was not and could not be the case – the destruction was too random, some things thrown away from them and some things towards, some to the left of where the fire had been, and some to the right. The pattern was too random to be anything but human design.

His filing cabinets were on their sides, looking as though someone had pried them open with a crowbar. Whoever had done it hadn't even bothered to go at it from the front and pry open each drawer – they had ripped open the whole side of it, opening it like a turkey and unveiling its innards. Several of his computers were smashed, both the towers and monitors. The towers she understood, but all smashing the monitors did was scatter plastic and liquid crystal everywhere. The monitors told her that, on some level, whomever had done this had revelled in the destruction.

Gamgee's desk projector – which he used to display the maps to the locations he sent her to in 3D – had taken the most damage. The entire surface of it was smashed, and even now it was attempting to display a security warning but it was so cracked and garbled that only a few pixels of it floated in the air above – so few that she hadn't even noticed them until she started looking for them.

"Thank you," Gamgee said, finally catching his breath and fixing his glasses back up onto his nose. "I hate those things."

"What happened here?"

"We've had an intruder," Gamgee said matter-of-factly. He nodded to the security camera in the far corner of the ceiling and pulled his tablet out of his bag as he spoke to her. It started booting up.

"Did they get anything? Any of the artifacts?" Her voice was suddenly panicked. She thought of the vial of cold-infected dream dust she'd taken from Cephalon, and how it had almost become an incurable, deadly version of itself. The cold-infused dream dust, in the wrong hands, could be devastating and she felt the colour drain from her cheeks as she considered the consequences of it. Consequences that would, ultimately, be her own fault.

Before he could answer, she made her way to one of the locked refrigeration units where they kept the sample and started trying her code.

"I'll know in just a moment," Gamgee said, the tablet having finally booted up and now loading his security feed from the secure server.

Cassidy ignored him, trying desperately instead to remember and input a four-digit code she never used. She slipped twice, and on the third time got it, hearing the lock slide out, and she pulled on the handle.

The sample was there, the blue powder resting comfortably in its tube. It glowed just from the shaking of her opening the fridge, and she breathed a sigh of relief.

"Got it," Gamgee said, even as the recorded sounds of the lab's destruction started to play over the tablet's speakers. There were crashes and grunts as whomever was doing it – a male, by the voice – pushed over the filing cabinet and bisected it and began spilling its files out into the air.

Cassidy walked back up to where Gamgee was standing, slower now. It was less urgent now that she knew the dream dust was safe. She stepped up beside him and looked over his shoulder at the security feed, and suddenly her mouth was dry.

The man on the feed was the man who had been talking to Rica at the mall – dark hair tossing about through the effort of his actions, black shirt, and big, thick black military boots. As if to confirm, he ran his crowbar along the table projector and then carried the motion through to look up at the security camera, meeting her gaze through the gap of time between them just as they had locked eyes in the mall. He was sneering, but there was a smile peeking at the corners of his lips – he was angry, but he was enjoying this.

"I know him," Cassidy said, her voice hushed. She sounded upset in a way she never did, and it got Gamgee's attention and made him raise a bushy eyebrow at her. "I saw him at the mall today, flirting with Rica."

Gamgee winced and looked like he was about to object to that assessment of the situation, then thought better of it. "You're sure it's the same person?" he said.

Cassidy watched as the man broke eye contact with

the camera, then turned and used the bar to crack open Gamgee's desk and pull out the drawers. "Very sure."

As they watched, the man in black pulled a small box out of Gamgee's desk and opened it. He took something out, a small metal stick that looked similar to a USB drive, and examined it. He smiled, so broadly that Cassidy could see the skin of his cheeks push up even from the side.

He turned and held the device up to the camera, smiled at them, and saluted. He put it safely into his pocket, picked up his crowbar again, then continued his destruction.

"What was that?" Cassidy asked. The device had looked familiar, but the grain on the feed made it hard to tell exactly what it had been.

"The Digital Heart," Gamgee frowned. "He took the Digital Heart you brought back from Dead World."

# CHAPTER FOUR

Preston Cane was slow to pack anything into his overnight bag. He was always slow at things he was told to do or had to do: it was one of the great flaws of him. Even as her sisters were making sure they'd packed their toiletries and zipping up, Preston Cane was still deciding between the merits of tube socks versus no-shows.

Cassidy huffed, marching over to him. "Stop it, that doesn't matter." She snatched the tube socks from his hand and shoved them into his bag with force. "You're just going to the hotel. Have fun, relax by the pool, have a drink. Don't... don't think too much about it."

"Can you at least tell me which hotel we're going to?" he asked, warbling. "Or how many pairs I'll need?"

She frowned and reached into his dresser drawer and scooped up a handful of socks and shoved them all in.

He regarded her cautiously, but nodded.

"That's actually a good point," Margo said, stepping into the doorway with her bag over her shoulder. Rica was in the hall behind her. "Where the hotel is really dictates what I'm taking. Like, if it's the one outside the city limits,

I'm definitely bringing my swim gear, but if it's the one with the outlet mall attached, forget that."

"It's..." Cassidy started with a whispered hiss, then stopped herself, eyeing the corners of the room as though there were ears waiting and listening in on what she was about to say. She stopped. When she spoke again her voice was sterner, yet more defeated. "Just get your things ready, please."

Margo raised an eyebrow, then turned back to Rica. She patted her bag. "We are ready... what's up?"

"Nothing," she frowned, getting several of her father's shirts from the closet and then bringing them to his bag and laying them in, folded. "Just... get your things. And where's Mom?"

"I texted her. She's finishing up at the Farmers' Market, she'll be back soon," Margo said. She shrugged and stepped out of the doorway towards the hall to collect her pool shoes, just in case they were being put up in the hotel outside the city.

Rica stopped Cassidy, putting out a hand so that it caught her sister by the crook of her arm as she walked by. "You said you wanted to be closer," she said, her voice level and matter-of-fact, speaking more like Cassidy than herself for a moment. She spoke as though she were channelling wisdom from beyond her years. "Being closer means being honest."

Preston and Margo both stopped what they were doing and turned from Rica to Cassidy.

Cassidy frowned, pursing her lips. "You know that work I've been doing for Dr. Gamgee?"

They nodded.

"It's not always... safe. I know that a lot of what I've done in my life hasn't been strictly 'safe,' but sometimes this work has the potential to get very, very unsafe." She paused, waiting for them to ask questions. When none came, she continued. "Last night there was a break-in at his office. Some guy... he trashed the place. He stole something I'd recovered on an expedition. Something we were still... cataloguing."

Rica tilted her head, catching the hesitation and knowing that it meant her sister wasn't being totally forthright with her, but deciding that whatever bit she was holding back wasn't salient to the story. Being honest didn't always mean giving everything. "And?"

"On the security footage... it was the guy you met at the mall. The older one that was flirting with you."

Preston stopped what he was doing and turned to Rica with eyebrows raised to their apex. Margo did the same. "Pardon?"

"He wasn't flirting," Rica insisted. Then she let it go, that wasn't the point. "You're sure it was him? Not just your brain filling in missing details with someone else you just saw?"

"I'm sure. Dark hair, coming down in front of his face like an anti-hero from a manga. Dark shirt, jeans, athletic. Strong jaw, my height."

Margo bobbed her eyebrows. "Are we sure we don't want him to have been flirting?"

"This is serious," Cassidy stressed. "It's not a coincidence that he was at the lab and around you. That's a Venn diagram with not a lot of overlap: it's basically me. So we need to assume he's messing my life up for some reason and get you guys to–"

"I met a young man the other day that fit that description," Preston interrupted, his voice hollow and far away. "He seemed nice."

Cassidy stared at him. "You see? This isn't okay. We've got to get to the hotel now. And I don't want to say which one, just on the off-chance... that he's listening. Somehow." They stared at her. She huffed. "You're not being paranoid if somebody really is out to get you."

Rica frowned at that logic for a moment, then reluctantly nodded. She stepped into the room to help her father get the last of his clothes ready. Margo joined as well.

"Thank you," Cassidy smiled, letting out a sigh. She pulled her phone out of her pocket and started to dial. "Now we just need to figure out where Mom is."

She put the phone to her ear and listened to it ring. A few seconds later, on the nightstand, her mother's ringtone called out to them. All four of them turned to stare at it.

*** 

Kayla Cane walked through the lanes at the Plainsfield Farmers' Market with a wide smile on her face. She had just found the perfect tomato: round and firm, and about the size of a baseball. It was so perfect she almost didn't want to use it later, but would.

Walking in time with her, several feet behind, was a tall man with dark hair and a dark shirt. He had a strong jaw, and his eyes followed Kayla wherever she went.

# CHAPTER FIVE

"Excuse me?" Tallis asked, stepping up behind Kayla and putting a gentle hand on her shoulder. "I think this was yours." He held out a gold necklace to her, its chain wrapped around each of his lanky fingers for stability.

The necklace was one that she'd been looking at a moment before, at a table several slots away. The vendor was a jeweller that made pieces by trapping flowers in resin – her booth was lined with dead foliage, contained in suspended animation at the moment of their demise, each petal smoothed out until it blossomed for whomever came near. This one in particular was a Lithodora, the starkness of its deep blue faded by the resin it was encased in, but the yellow at its centre as bright as the midday sun.

Kayla stared at it for just a moment, then smiled and turned her kind eyes towards the man. She noticed the strange jewelry along the side of his face – shimmering gold, with small crystals. It was hard to turn away from the necklace to look at him, actually. The piece had called her so readily when she'd been at the booth that it had been a struggle to turn away from it. She'd wondered –

and not for the first time – what it was in humans that called them to certain objects, especially when there was little logic in the exchange. She had touched it, even, but then stepped away from it. Despite the strange pull it had on her, she knew that it was frivolous.

She stared at it now again, at how the light caught the edge of the resin and yet also lit the flower within. "No," she said finally, forcing herself to look past it to the man holding it. He transfixed her for a moment, too. "I didn't drop that, I'm sorry."

"I didn't say you dropped it, I said it was yours," he said, his voice smooth like silk. He stepped around to be behind her, asking permission with his motion, and she nodded. He placed the necklace around her, clasping it with deft fingers. It was even the right size, hanging below her collarbones and looking like it had always been there. He stepped back around to see it on her, like an artist admiring his work. "There, you see? I knew it. Yours."

She touched its edge again, just as she had when she'd been admiring it, then stepped back to the mirror that the vendor had set up. It did look perfect on her, just as she'd imagined it would. There were some things in life that disappointed – that never looked the same on the rack as they did in real life: jeans, shoes, and shirts with full-body prints – but this was exactly the same on as it had been in her mind's eye. She stared at it and the reflection of her with it for a long moment, as though seeing herself complete for the first time. Tallis was behind her and she could see his reflection over her own shoulder. "Really, I shouldn't," she protested one last time, but without conviction.

"Please," he said, and she heard his voice become unsteady despite his smile. "I saw it and saw you looking at it and I knew that it was meant to be yours. Please."

Kayla smiled, then nodded and stepped away from the mirror.

Tallis smiled at her for a long moment, then a startled expression came over him as though he had become aware that he might have let the moment linger too long. He coughed into his fist then turned and motioned to the market. "It's a lovely place. And a lovely day for it. Do you come here often?"

"I do," Kayla smiled. "I used to come with my children, although my oldest hated it."

"I can't imagine that's true."

"Ooooh, it is. She used to beg and scream to be free of it. It got to the point that I'd try bribing her with treats or food or toys from the vendors, but she wouldn't have it. When she got old enough I started leaving her home with her books instead."

Tallis shook his head, smiling.

"Did they have Farmers' Markets where you're from...?"

His smile faded for a moment, and when it returned it was a wistful smirk. "Yes, actually. They did. I used to enjoy going to them with my mother very, very much. When she was alive."

"Do they have butt-kicking where you're from?" came a voice from behind them. "Because if not, I'd be happy to introduce you to the concept."

Tallis turned, revealing that Cassidy had stepped up behind them. Her shoulders were already squared and ready, her body tilted towards him to make her frame as small a target as possible if he chose to strike. His smile widened as he saw her, travelling totally up one side of his cheek. "Why hello."

"Cassidy?" Kayla asked, confused. "What're you doing here?" She noticed her daughter's aggressive stance and recognized it from years of karate training. "What's going on?"

"Get out of here, Mom," Cassidy said, not taking her gaze away from Tallis for an instant to regard her. She stared at the Branch of Languages that ran along his cheek and recognized it for what it was and what it meant, and some of the colour drained from her. "Go back to the house. Dad's waiting for you."

"What're you—"

"I know what this must look like," Tallis cooed, putting both his hands up with palms open in a 'calm down' gesture that could have all too easily become aggressive at a moment's notice. "But I swear, there's nothing sinister happening here."

"Who is this?" Kayla asked, stepping back away from both of them.

"He destroyed Gamgee's lab," Cassidy said matter-of-factly. "Stole something. He's been after me, and he was stalking Rica and Dad."

Kayla turned to him, sympathy transforming completely into anger in one fell swoop. "You did what?"

Tallis turned away from Cassidy, the angered glare seeming to shake him. He pursed his lips and turned back, now glaring with new anger at Cassidy. "This isn't what it looks like. I'm not 'after you.'"

"You could have fooled me."

He sighed. "Why don't you ask Gamgee why I was there?"

"You were there for the Digital Heart."

"No. Yes... but, no." He smirked. He was starting to enjoy this, and started to step around her in a wide circle. She adjusted her stance towards him in increments, always keeping the smallest part of herself facing him.

"How'd you find me?"

"Actually, I have a better question. Because the answer to it also answers the 'why I was at Gamgee's lab' question, and I like it when one thing answers two questions. I like the symmetry of it. It always seems... planned. So here it is: how... did he find you?"

Cassidy stopped turning to meet him, the unexpected question shaking her a little. She stiffened, breaking her stance. "What do you mean?"

He stopped stepping around her, smiling. He was a full one-hundred and eighty degrees from where he had started, in relation to her. "I mean exactly that. How did Gamgee find you? Every question you have, that question also answers. That is the whole thing."

"Then tell me it."

He smiled. "It'll be better if it comes from him." He said the last word with venom in his voice, then turned quickly and ran towards the exit. It was only then that Cassidy realized that he had circled her until he was closer to it than she was.

"Dang it!" she hissed, then started after him.

"Cassidy, stop!" her mother yelled.

She did so, turning back to her, wedged between the

two forces pulling her for a long moment. After only an instant or two of hesitation, the waiting made her choice for her, as Tallis' lead and steady run made the gap between them insurmountable. She cursed through her teeth, then turned back to her mother.

"Take this," she said, slapping her own phone into her mother's hands. "Call Dad; you left your phone at the house. Don't let him off the line the whole time until you join him, just in case something happens."

"What was that about?" Kayla demanded, gripping the bobble on the end of her necklace as though it were now a talisman.

"I don't know," Cassidy admitted, lowering her eyes at Tallis as he vanished from view. "But I am going to find out."

# CHAPTER SIX

Cassidy slammed her hands down on the broken projection table in Gamgee's office, making him jump and strike his head on it from underneath. The attack had shorted out the mechanism underneath that made the entire thing function, and he had been desperately trying to repair it when she'd come in. She'd never taken note of it before, but it looked as though there were ARC crystals helping run the mechanism.

"How did you find me?" she asked, her tone sharp and accusatory.

He rubbed his bald head and grunted as he pulled himself out from under the table. "Pardon?"

"I met the man who did this today," she said, motioning to the destruction around her. "He was following my mother. Who knows what would have happened if I hadn't shown up."

"Nothing would have happened."

"He was wearing a Branch of Languages, Gamgee," Cassidy stressed. "And he told me to ask you how you found me. He said that that would answer all my questions, even the ones I hadn't asked yet."

Gamgee stared at her for a long moment, rubbing his head to dull the pain of his bruise at first and then moving down to stroke the back of his neck in a move she'd rarely seen him do: one that displayed anxiety. He frowned, clearing his throat. "You weren't the first adventurer I worked with. The first person who hopped between worlds for me."

Her eyebrows raised and the colour left her cheeks. She felt her jaw work itself into a tight hinge and felt her palms resting on the broken glass of the projector curl up into fists, but she said nothing. She stared at him, waiting for him to continue without giving him the satisfaction of beckoning him to.

"Some time ago now, I was approached by a young man who said he was from another world. He called himself Tallis. I thought he was crazy." Gamgee smirked a little. "He was young and he was brash, and I thought the whole thing was a scam, honestly. But the more I talked to him... the more I started to believe it. That there could be holes between worlds." He stared wistfully off into the distance for a moment, remembering what it was like to discover that truth for the first time. "He told me that he'd found me because he'd come from a world where my life was different. Where I'd become a biologist, and not a physicist. A world where I'd cured McMillon disease."

She swallowed, straightening. "You didn't bring back the cure?"

"No, but I did discover it. Not in this reality, but it was 'me.' I took some solace in that when I was accepting my accolades and credit and praise. It was me, just a different version of me."

"He's not from that world, though. The one I went through. His English was too perfect to be the product of the Branch of Languages."

"No, we found that world later. It had an even better adaptation of the cure. It's timeline was more accelerated than ours, it's civilization had started earlier. They were further ahead in some medical breakthroughs than us, so when we found it we adapted their cure into the one Tallis had brought from the other me." He smiled. "He thought only I could understand my own work enough to reverse engineer it. He was right."

She did not smile back at him. "What happened then?"

Gamgee stared at her for a long moment, then swallowed. "Then... he decided to stay. His world wasn't a home to him anymore, but he had this device," Gamgee motioned to his wrist watch, "that he'd picked up on another world that could let him know where other portals were. Together we mapped out... most of the portals that we know the locations of."

Cassidy looked up at where the projection of the map usually hovered, as if expecting it to be there upon mention even though the screen was broken.

"We worked together, just like you and I did. Getting technology and cures and information from other worlds that could help us, here. Everything was fine... until one day, he went through a portal and didn't come back."

Cassidy swallowed, locking eyes with him. "What did you do?"

"Nothing. I'd... assumed, honestly, that he'd moved

on. That he'd found another world to call home, or that he'd just grown tired of the chase. He and I didn't have the same relationship we do, it was always strained. Always hard. We bickered, a lot. When he didn't come back, I'd assumed he'd had enough of it."

Cassidy nodded, looking away and thinking about this. She squinted. "What was he looking for?"

"Hm?"

"What was he after, the last time you saw him?"

Gamgee turned back to the opaque crystals that helped run the projector he was trying to fix. "ARC crystals."

Cassidy's jaw went slack. "You abandoned him on Xik'en? A planet that's hostile to mammals? To humans?"

"I didn't know that, then." He sighed.

"He wasn't in retirement, he'd probably spent all that time rotting in an Xik'en prison cell!"

"I didn't know that, then," he reiterated.

She squinted. "But you knew it when I came back. When I came back from the Bermuda Triangle portal and gave my report, you knew it then. You knew what that world was like and what probably happened there and you chose not to tell me or do anything about it, even then."

Gamgee pursed his lips in shame, then nodded.

Cassidy cursed, turning away from him and placing her hands on her hips. She stayed like that for a long time, then turned to face him from over her shoulder. "That doesn't explain how you found me."

# CHAPTER SEVEN

Tallis sat among the discarded circuitry and technology of his workspace, sparks illuminating his stark features as he soldered a new wire into the board in front of him. It was long and green, with several rows of transistors lining one side that he'd placed to feed back from the current and through a rewired USB port he had attached to the side opposite him. There was a second on the side closest – this one a micro-USB – that fed out into a series of uninsulated wires. Those wires travelled in a spiral around his arm and came to a head connected into the glowing wristwatch he had on his left arm.

He made several adjustments to the soldering, keeping the screen of his watch for any warning signs as he did, but nothing had illuminated it yet.

The chair he was on had been salvaged from a scrap yard, as had many of the circuit boards and screens and terminals. There was a mattress on the floor behind him with no blankets or bedding on it, not that any was needed: the basement he was in was hot. He sweated at night, surrounded by the teetering towers of technology. The home he was in was vacant and for sale, and had been on the market for quite some time. Nobody would notice him there, but he couldn't risk being upstairs in case a nosey neighbour saw him through the window and called the owners or the police.

The chair was not comfortable and neither was the bed, but both were far and above more comforting than a Xik'en penitentiary, and so he had slept some of the best, more restful sleeps of his life. The Xik'en, he had come to learn, were not believers in 'reform' when it came to mammals: only incarceration and punishment.

He soldered the last wire in place, and suddenly the screen on his watch came to life. It cycled through all the different colours it could make – red, green, blue, yellow, and purple – before doing them all again and settling on its "default positive" of red for a moment. He smiled. He didn't understand this world, where green meant something positive. His screen flashed red, meaning it had accepted the wiring, and he smiled.

Tallis reached into his pocket and produced the Digital Heart. He carefully plugged it into the wires coming from the altered USB slot on the side away from him and turned back to the screen.

He looked at another screen to his right. It showed a digital map of Plainsfield, and a blinking light that read Cassidy on the dot that represented a hotel on the edge of the city.

As if by magic, the firmware of the Digital Heart interacted with that of the alien device and started to repair it. He watched it flicker through diagnostics, ones and zeros fluttering over the screen as it improved itself based on the Heart's base programming, and he smiled.

When it was done he pressed a button on either side of the watch at once, and this time when the screen lit up it projected a small hologram into the air above his wrist. He swiped through the air of it and found that he could interact with it again, like a smartphone, and grinned.

He scrolled through his apps until he found the call feature, then selected Gamgee's name from the list of contacts.

\*\*\*

Cassidy cursed, turning away from him and placing her hands on her hips. She stayed like that for a long time, then turned to face him from over her shoulder. "That doesn't explain how you found me."

There was a loud beeping sound from under the table then, and the few projection lights that were still working started to sputter to life.

Gamgee turned and stepped over to the exposed terminal, where the ARC crystals were glowing to life.

"What's happening?" Cassidy asked, stepping up to the screen as an image started to form.

"Someone's calling."

"It can accept calls?"

As if in answer, Tallis appeared in a blue projection hovering over the table. There were spots of him missing as not all the projection bulbs were functioning, but it seemed as though something on Tallis' side was working to compensate for that. He was much larger than he should have been, only his bust visible and appearing at close to five times his actual size.

"Hello, can you hear me?" Tallis said. The giant figure reached out and tapped something in front of him, and the entire image shimmered and fluttered away and produced a blunt -tunk tunk- sound. "I can't see you or hear you, but that makes sense. I'm assuming you can see me."

Gamgee stepped up close to the shimmering blue giant, his mouth agape.

"I met the new version. She's nice, she's got spunk, I've gotta say. Nothing wrong with how she was raised, I'll say that."

"Why is he talking about me like that?" Cassidy asked.

"He doesn't know you're here. My setup isn't set up to make calls, he's just hacked into the projection system. Like when you video call someone that doesn't have a camera or microphone attached."

"You guys do good work," Tallis continued, licking his lips. "And you should keep doing good work... but not off of my blood, sweat, and tears, Gamgee." He paused. "I want my work, Gamgee. And all the work that's come from my work. Fruit of the poisonous tree, and all that. I deserve it all, and I want it all. In fact I'd like you to meet me at Plainsfield Park today at five to produce it. You'll know the spot." He stopped for a moment, then smiled magnanimously. "I have no desire to shut you down. This is not about revenge," he said, in a tone that left no doubt that it was, mostly, about revenge. "I just want to start up on my own, like I would have if I hadn't met you. I want you out of my life, want to start fresh." He frowned, then reached for the screen again. "And if you don't, I'll burn your whole world down to get it. I'm sorry. See you at five."

The projection blinked off, and all of the lights that still worked around the table disengaged.

"He wants all the work," Gamgee said, his voice hushed. "His work and everything based on it? That's everything. He wants to take everything from me."

Cassidy laughed ruefully. "I mean it doesn't sound like you don't deserve it. Lying. Keeping secrets. Leaving a man in a Xik'en prison. These don't sound like things people do when they don't want their work taken from them."

Gamgee turned on her. "You don't know what you're saying. He's not like me, Cassidy. We fought, often and always. He doesn't want the research to help mankind – he wants money. When he brought the cure for McMillon disease, he wanted to patent it, charge for it. Not a lot... not an insane, ten-thousand percent markup... but enough that he would have been one of the richest men in the world."

Cassidy looked around the large laboratory. "You seem to have done alright for yourself."

"Off grants. Off awards. And all of it, you'll notice, right back into the project. If I give him everything, that all changes. All of it."

She paused for a long moment, lips still tight. She was still angry with him. She nodded.

# CHAPTER EIGHT

Tallis stood in the middle of the open field portion of the Plainsfield Park, people playing Frisbee and catch all around him. He stood in one spot and never swayed, like a high tower in an open field, the energy of the evening park happening all around him. It was chaos, but a controlled chaos, and he watched it all with a warm smile on his face as people ran and yelled and laughed. All the while, they ignored him. It was like he wasn't even there.

The Branch of Languages hugged the side of his jaw and caught the light from the lowering sun, making it shimmer. Despite the fact that it sparkled and vied for attention, nobody paid it any. He remembered, briefly, that on his home world if someone had worn something so plainly audacious it would have earned them stares and glares and ridicule. He wondered if the lack of attention the Branch was being paid was due to the changes that made this dimension unique... or simply the natural passage of time and the increased acceptance of different things.

It occurred to his wandering mind that many, many

years had passed since he had last stepped foot on his 'own' Earth, and that in the time since, things might have changed. Culture would have changed, and trends and fads. Politics would have certainly changed, both on a micro level and a broader, global level. It was entirely possible that, given the changes and the time he'd been away, there was no longer any Earth that would feel familiar to him. That 'home' was something he would only ever be able to feel again in nostalgia.

"You were on the call as well, I take it?" he said, a slow smirk growing over his features. He turned around and his gaze found Cassidy, who had been approaching from behind him from across the field. She was now ten feet away, and stopped suddenly when he laid eyes on her. There was something about his eyes that made her pull to a stop, every time.

"I was," she said definitively.

He chuckled humourlessly, looking up at the sky. "I should have known. I tracked your phone and I thought – I thought – that, given the perceived threat to your family, that you'd stay with them. Comfort them, give them hugs and normalcy... but I should have known better, shouldn't I have? Of course you were with Gamgee. I don't know how I thought you'd be anywhere else."

She paused, her step hesitant. When she took another step towards him he made one away, his first.

"Gamgee told me what you want to do with the research," she said in a matter-of-fact tone. "You want to exploit it, for profit."

He chuckled. "You're an idealist, I get that. Tell me: when doctors take a pay check for performing a heart transplant, are they being exploitative? Hm? What about grocery clerks, stocking shelves? Are they exploiting the people who pay them?"

"That's not the same."

"You seem to think it is. You seem to want to paint a picture where getting paid a proper rate for my work is wrong, when really it incentivizes me to do more of my work. If my work is valuable to mankind then they should pay me for the pleasure, as simple as that."

"Some things, sure. That bobble on the side of your face," she motioned along the side of her own face to indicate the Branch of Languages on his. "But not things like cures for diseases. Not things like the McMillon disease cure."

Tallis laughed ruefully, but there wasn't joy in it. She thought she might have even saw tears forming in his eyes before he pushed them away. "Because you care about your family. Your father."

She straightened. "Yes."

"Your family that you never see. You're always out on your adventures – on other worlds, other planets, other dimensions – never once back here. Not long enough to see what's happening." He licked his lips. "How far was your father along into Stage Two before you noticed?"

She balked and swallowed, but said nothing.

"Or did you have to be told to notice? You spend so little time with them. Rica, she's grown up while you weren't even looking, and now you'll never get those years back. She's going to the same university you teach at, but I bet she doesn't want you to let anyone know about your connection."

"She wants to make it on her own merit," Cassidy snapped, forgetting herself and then recomposing herself.

"She's had to get by on her own merit, thus far, because you weren't there. Now she doesn't want you involved at the tail end. She's made it all this way without your help, without you being there, why would she want you stamping your name on the credit now, after all this time?"

Cassidy's eyebrows furrowed. She thought for a long moment, then shook her head. "It's not like that."

He met her eyes. "Don't pretend it's not. You chase the thrill, I know the type. I was the same. Not much excuse to get your blood pumping at Family Game Night, so why bother, right?"

"I went to Family Game Nights every week while Rica and Margo were growing up, thanks."

"But were you really there?" he squinted. "Were you there in your head? Or were you off somewhere else, your mind on some adventure while you tapped the piece along the board like a zombie?"

Cassidy nodded, pursing her lips and swallowing. "I'm sorry about what happened to you on Xik'en," she said, changing the topic with confidence in her voice. "I really am. That place was awful. I only survived it because I had a friend there. I can't imagine what it would have been like to have been there without one."

Tallis' lip curled. "You don't deserve them, you know. The friends. The family. You don't appreciate them and they stick by you and they will until it's over, but you don't deserve them." His pale cheeks were growing red and hot.

"You seem like you're getting angrier at me than you are at Gamgee."

He paused, considered that with a sneer on his face, then nodded. "That is... accurate. Yes."

She thought for a moment, then stepped forward. This time he did not step back. "Maybe you'd like to have it out then? Decide this like adventurers, winner take all?"

"By all, do you mean the research?"

"I do."

"Then. I. Agree." He said each word clipped, like they were each their own sentence. "Where?"

"There's a beach five miles from the outer edge of Plainsfield, with evergreen trees and brush all around it. It continues to the edge of the continent, then suddenly drops off into large, tanned boulders. You've never seen boulders like these. They're laid there like toys a toddler was done playing with. You can hear the waves crash there, can feel the surf against your skin."

"I know the place," he nodded. "Bring the files."

She nodded, and he turned and marched away from her again, but this time she made no effort to catch him, she merely watched him go with a steely resolve in her eyes.

# CHAPTER NINE

Cassidy burst through the doors of Gamgee's lab, already running toward the line of locked refrigeration units. Gamgee stood up from his repairs quickly, avoiding striking his head this time, and spun around to watch her. "Cassidy? What are you doing?"

She did not answer, instead finding her way to the third fridge in and trying her four-digit code. She got it on the first try and pulled the door open to the hiss of air and plumes of cold condensation.

The sample was there, the blue powder resting comfortably in its tube. It glowed just from the shaking of her opening the fridge, and she stared at it with a stern, resigned expression.

It was the cold-infected dream dust from Cephalon.

Gamgee's face lost colour and he took a step towards her. "What are you planning on doing with that?"

"What I have to."

# CHAPTER TEN

Tallis followed the tracks that had been left in the tall grass before him, leading away from the crumbling road and the dense plot of evergreen trees and down to the very edge of the continent, suddenly dropping off into large, tanned boulders. They came together haphazardly and yet with great purpose, but most were firmly in place after an age of time and pressure. They formed caves that dotted the shoreline, lined with kelp and small shellfish. The tide was out, but it was clear that at another day or time the caves might have been hip deep with crashing waves.

On the air he could hear the steady clap of work, like thunder on the open air. There would be a large snap, and then several seconds. He knew what it was by the sound of it, but didn't know why it was. He came off the steep boulders onto the relative flatness of the shore, a brief edge of ten feet that bordered the last edge of the world before disappearing into the oblivion of the sea. The waves were such a deep blue they were nearly black, like ink pushing its way towards the unspent parchment of the forest. They crashed and rolled, leaving creamy foam in the crevices and cracks of the stone.

There were several caves in the cliffside, holes that came to sharp points at the top and bottom, widening into foot-long gaps at their middles. They gaped like maws, small breaks in reality where light had no place. There were several of them in varying shapes and sizes, some appearing more inhabitable by an adult human form than others. One of them was elevated slightly above the rest, and Cassidy was at its mouth.

She was thick with sweat that covered her face, and had been there so long that it had begun to dry on and have a new layer come in its wake. It was soaked into her shirt under her arms, her jacket off and her suspenders showing. Her mouth was open with the stress and heat of it, and she had a pickaxe in her hands. She was chiselling away at the slender gap of the cave, making it wider and wider. It was where the thunderclap had come from, the pause as she caught her breath, the anticipation between them.

He stepped up to her, slowly, and she saw him coming out of the corner of her eye. She stopped her work, wiped her brow with her bare arm, then opened a bottle of ice water that had been resting at her side. She drank it all, every last bit of it.

"This isn't what I expected to find," Tallis said, slowly closing the gap between them.

She swallowed, then motioned for him to stop and turn around.

There was a bear walking along the edge of a steep ridge of the cliff, its fur barely visible between the trees but clearly there all the same. It ate berries the way only a bear could, entire branches of the bush finding their way into its mouth and then being strained through clenched, sharpened teeth when it pulled back. It ignored them, far enough away that neither party was a danger to the other. It was used to humans. Even this far into the wild, there was no wilderness.

"That is beautiful," he said, admiring it.

"I saw one just like that the first time I was out here," Cassidy mused, stepping away from her work. She slid on her bomber jacket, which had been resting on the stone next to her, and suddenly looked clean.

Tallis raised an eyebrow at her, noticing the lack of bullet holes or scrapes. "New jacket?"

She splayed out her arms and held them aloft, looking from arm to arm as though she were just noticing it for the first time. She had made two stops after she'd gone to see Gamgee, and one of them had been back to the store she had visited right before she saw Tallis for the first time. She had gone back and this time she had taken the coat off the rack without hesitation, marched right to the register and paid for it. Her old, torn coat was back in her car, thrown over the back seat like an animal carcass and with just as many bullet holes in it. This one still smelled of new, the oils in it reaching her nostrils even as she raised them. "Yeah. I thought it was about time."

"Do you have the files?" he asked, his voice losing some of its conversational impishness.

She reached to her breast pocket and unbuckled it, the new clasp coming loose with difficulty. She fished her entire hand in and came back with a thick jump drive, connector cables dangling from it. She kept its front facing him, the symbol of the big tech firm that made it glimmering in the light of the setting sun.

"You expect me to believe that's the only copy?"

"Does it need to be the only copy? Once you patent what's on it, it doesn't matter what we do."

He squinted. "I don't want competition."

"I'll magnetize any copies we have if you win. Which, you won't. So let's not bother arguing about the logistics of how something will work that's never going to happen for too long, okay?"

He smirked. "You know I'm going to win. We always win. And I know that you know I'm going to win... because if you didn't, you wouldn't have brought the drive at all."

She shuffled on her feet, her eyes flitting back to the hole in the rock she had been working at. There was water coming from it, like a small freshwater stream that joined the ocean a little ways down the beach. It was like freshwater, and all logic stated it should be freshwater, but she knew that if she bent and took a mouthful of it, that it would be salt. She did not respond to his taunt, just set her jaw and stared at him.

"So how are we going to do this?" he asked, stepping around her in a slow arc, just as he had at the Farmers' Market. He motioned towards the lapping waves. "Will we fight to the death up to our ankles in sea foam, wrestling and both getting soaked and cold?" He paused and smirked. "That would certainly be dramatic, and I'd be lying if I said I'd never wondered what a fight like that would turn out like."

"That's not really my style," she replied, each word clipped. She had closed her fists until her knuckles were white, her right once wrapped around the frame of the drive.

He stopped walking and regarded her, looking her up and down as if appraising her as a fighter. "It's really not, is it? I can see that you can fight, but you don't actually fight much. How do you get out of all those precarious situations we tend to find ourselves in, if that's the case?"

"My brain, mostly," she grinned. "You should try it, sometime."

"Oh, hoho," he laughed heartily. "I'm quite smart, I'll have you know. Top of my class. Much like you, I'd imagine. Maybe in different areas... but still the top. Still the overachiever, the over-exceller. We're a type."

"If you were smart you wouldn't have come at me through my family."

He stopped at that, his face changing from smugness to slackness, as though the statement had taken him aback. "For that last time, I wasn't coming at you through them."

"It had a funny way of looking like that."

"I lost my family," he said, his voice too cold and hurt for any of it to be lies. "I'm sorry if I was feeling... nostalgic isn't the word, but it's close enough. I miss mine, but that didn't give me the right to intrude on yours. I honestly apologize."

She straightened. She had not expected that. "You come at me through my family to get this intel, and then you apologize?"

"As hard as it might be for you to believe, those two

things were not linked."

She squinted.

He swallowed hard, then motioned back to the surf with a broad gesture. "So, what then? If we're not going to duke it out in the water, where?" He was standing at the sea's edge now, the waves licking at the heels of his thick black boots. "Maybe on those rocks you were chipping away at? We could fight like Kirk and the Gorn on that episode of Star Trek." He paused. "Did they have Star Trek, here? I've never looked."

She nodded.

"Amazing the things that are the same. In two worlds, that one little series ran for forty seasons, even with all the differences between us. That's amazing, when you think about it."

She opened her mouth to correct him, then closed it. It wasn't the point. "We're not going to fight."

"Oh? I don't see how you plan on this ending then. Because I hate to be the person who gives bad news, but I will fight. I will absolutely fight. I will fight you and Gamgee and anyone else he recruits to stand in my way to get the work I'm owed." He stepped toward her, and she stepped back toward the slender cave. Her feet almost slipped on the uneven rock, but she steadied herself. He sighed. "You can't keep putting this off. How will it end then?"

"I told you. I'll do the smart thing," she said, holding up the drive with its front toward him again. "And give you the drive."

Before he could respond she had lobbed it through the air at him, throwing it like an underhand baseball pitch that was intended to be hit. The drive went up and then swiftly back down to earth in a narrow arc, and he knew instinctively that it would come short of him and shatter on the rocks, all his work lost forever.

He dove quickly, reaching out both cupped hands and catching the drive even as Cassidy turned and stepped away from him. The drive fell into his waiting arms and bounced, and he snapped it tight to his chest to stop it from escaping and falling to the stone.

There was a sound of breaking glass, and suddenly his black shirt was streaked with shimmering blue dust. It swirled around him and up onto his face and into his nostrils when he gasped for air. He looked up at her, his eyes wide and somewhere between rage and fright and confusion.

She was standing at the mouth of the cave, with one foot propped up on the rock in front of it like the heroes from the old adventure serials.

Tallis looked down at the drive. On the back of it there had been a glass vial taped that had housed the blue dust that was now all over him and in him, streaking his face. "What is this?" he asked angrily.

"Cephalon dream dust," she said matter-of-factly.

He looked down at it, brushing it off his shirt and only succeeding in spreading it.

"I assume you've been to Cephalon?"

He nodded.

"That dream dust... has been fused with the common cold."

His eyes went wide. "What have you done?"

"It'll kill anyone with an imagination... and you have many faults, but I don't think a lack of imagination is one of them."

He staggered, his feet becoming rubber. "I thought you didn't do violence?"

"I don't," she smirked, then reached into her breast pocket again, producing a second vial. This one looked sturdier, like it was made of thick plastic, and it contained a clear liquid that looked like water. "You've never been to Lotus Lorea, have you?"

His brow furrowed.

"No, I found that one. I've been working, too. This is a small, diluted sample of the Lotus Fountain water. I kept it hidden from Gamgee... now I guess I know why. It cures anything." She looked at the vial, then at him. "Put down the drive."

He coughed, and a cloud of blue came from him that shook him. He glared at her... then put the drive down on the shore at his feet. If they stayed like they were, the tides would take them within minutes. "Give me the potion."

Cassidy smiled, nodded, then turned and brought the vial up high. "Catch!"

She threw it into the cave, its plastic so thick that they heard it bounce, and not break. It bounced twice and he was already on his feet, scrambling up the sharp incline of the shore and into the mouth of the cave.

She stepped down the shore quickly, in a wide circle away from him just as he had with her, so that he could not change tactics and attack her, then scooped up the drive just as the approaching tide was about to take it.

# CHAPTER ELEVEN

Tallis came out of the mouth of the cave back out onto the beach, even though he hadn't turned around. He'd ran into the cave after the sample of Lotus Fountain water and halfway through instead of getting closer to the wall he'd started out again. There was a ringing in his ears that he recognized at once was not in his head, but a high-pitched alarm.

Cassidy was no longer on the beach, and the day was brighter than it had been.

He gasped and looked around the beach, quickly examining the glint of every stone for the telltale sheen of plastic. The blue dust still clung to him, getting into the fabric of his shirt and in his hair and holding there.

He found the vial, nestled between two great stones and looking like it had always been there. He scooped it up, the clear liquid inside almost seeming to glow with promise. His thumb immediately started to work the cork out of the top, then he thought better of that. He stepped into the sea and let the crashing waves push around him, knocking the Dream Dust that was on his clothes off into the surf and diluting it beyond use. He dipped his head down into the sea of another world and got clean of it, then pushed himself back through the surface.

He stepped back towards the shore with that ringing in his ears getting louder.

He popped the cork top off the bottle and downed the sample of Lotus Fountain water that Cassidy had tossed away, feeling it tingle against his tongue and his throat as it made its way down. He drank it until it was gone, just in case.

He headed back towards the mouth of the cave.

Just as he was exiting the surf, a flying car appeared over the blind of the cliffside and elevated high into the air, shining a spotlight down onto him. Tallis dropped the empty bottle to the ground as three men in SWAT gear appeared over the ridge with their weapons raised.

Tallis turned from them to the mouth of the cave, knowing he couldn't reach it. He smirked. "Clever."

"Slipstreamer," the lead officer said with contempt, upon hearing Tallis' voice. "Put your hands on your face!"

Tallis' lip curled and he considered correcting the man on his grammar, then thought better of it. He put his hands on the top of his head and, when the officer told him to, lowered himself down to his knees. While he was doing so he kept the cave entrance in sight, and couldn't help but wear a smile on his face.

"Very clever."

# CHAPTER TWELVE

Cassidy wedged the thin, flat edge of her pickaxe into the scant crack at the bottom of the boulder next to the cave. She dug down into the sand a little more to give herself some leverage, then placed all her weight on the axe's handle and pushed down.

Her leverage did nothing at first and she screamed from the exertion of it, sweat forming from her every pore and streaming down her cheeks and off of her chin. The beach was hot and this made it hotter, but she could hear the distant sounds of yelling and it pressed her on. Could sound waves travel through the portal? She wasn't sure, but didn't see why not, and the uncertainty egged her on.

She let out a warrior's cry and gave one final heave of exertion, and finally the boulder moved. It rocked up on the axis of the axe at first, seeming to balance there in defiance of gravity and logic, before falling from its perch and tumbling down over to block the path.

She let out a sigh of relief, then fell from the rock elevation where the boulder had been into the sand below, her knees soaking in the last trickles of the stream of water from another world.

# CHAPTER THIRTEEN

Cassidy stepped into Gamgee's office in a way she never had before, with a resigned hesitation. He was at the far side, doing repairs on the inverter he'd been working on, and was partially obscured by its frame. She looked from side to side as she stepped towards him, at the panels of tech and cameras and lights that lined the walls, and for the first time it did not look impressive, it looked ominous.

The space was wide and open, cold both in temperature and emotionality, the light off the stainless steel instruments giving it an unearthly clean glow. Echoes were a constant in the space, so although he heard Cassidy enter the building long before she reached him, he'd made no effort to set down his work and address her until she was within five feet of him. When she was, he backed his way out from under the hood of the machine he was working on and forced a smile that she did not return. "You made it back."

"I did, yeah," she said with pursed lips. She took the jump drive with his work on it out of her breast pocket and pressed it down onto the terminal in the centre of the room with force, as though she thought that it would have gotten up and run away if she hadn't. "Would you have done anything for me if I hadn't?"

He looked at her and swallowed, unsure how to respond.

"That's... that's kind of what I thought." She tisked and shook her head.

"For you, I would have," he stressed, trying to sound sincere. "For an adventurer like you, I would have done whatever it took to get you back."

Her mouth became a thin line across her face and she shook her head. "I guess that's the thing, isn't it... no matter how exciting things are now... no matter how much they get my blood pumping... I just don't think these will feel like adventures anymore."

She took her hand off of the jump drive and turned her back on Gamgee, leaving it there and walking away from him.

Her footsteps echoed through the massive, empty hall. When she was halfway to the exit he called out after her: "You'll be back, won't you?"

Cassidy did not turn or respond in any way. She made her way to the exit, and out into the bright, natural light of the sunny day.

# CHAPTER FOURTEEN

"Can you pass the mash potatoes?" Preston asked, holding his hand out with the palm up and fingers splayed, ready to receive the bowl.

Cassidy smiled. The way he said 'mash potatoes' instead of 'mashed potatoes,' or any number of other small inflections that were uniquely him, always brought a fresh grin to her face.

She raised the blue swirled bowl of mashed potatoes like a ceremonial offering, then set it down with great weight on his waiting hand.

Everyone around the table laughed: Preston, Kayla, Margo and Rica. Rica laughed especially hard, while Margo seemed like she was just chuckling along. Margo didn't laugh involuntarily, often.

The dining room seemed to have grown since the last time she'd been in it, and become more welcoming. They all fit around it comfortably, passing food and utensils between each other with ease. The home seemed more welcoming than it had in years – for the first time in a long time, there was more of a tug to return to it than there was to the road or to the skies or to another world. For once, that ephemeral pull of destiny was bringing her back home, and she did not fight it.

Kayla sat at the far end of the table, eating edamame that had been drizzled in olive oil and topped with fresh black pepper. "So you're not working with Doctor Gamgee anymore?"

Cassidy turned to her. "No. Not anymore." She smiled.

"You'll have to get back to work here, then. Get a new grant, or something."

"Mom," Rica stressed, reaching out and touching the back of her mother's hand. "Money isn't everything."

Kayla bobbed her eyebrows as though she wasn't sure if that were true, but nodded in reluctant agreement.

Cassidy turned to look at her, only noticing now much Tallis' attitude had mirrored her mother's, in a strange way.

"We always win," Tallis had said, she remembered. And then later: "I lost my family" and "I wasn't coming at you through them."

The colour drained from Cassidy's cheeks, and after a moment Preston noticed and put a concerned hand on her arm. "Cass?"

Her mouth was dry, but she spoke. "You named me, right?"

He raised an eyebrow. "Pardon?"

"You named me?" She raised her gaze to meet his eye. "When I was born, you picked the name?"

"... Yes," he answered, drawing out the word. He looked across the table to Kayla. "We wanted something that meant 'clever.' We wanted you to be clever."

She nodded slowly. She turned to her mother. "What would you have named me if I'd been a boy?"

***

Tallis Cane woke in a holding cell with both arms chained to the solid concrete wall at a ninety degree angle. It was dark and he couldn't see the entire room, but he knew the smell of it, the taste of antiseptic in the back of his throat. There was no furniture or fixtures he could see, just bars along one side of the large cell and concrete walls on every other. It was private and yet as public as a panopticon, with anyone able to look into any corner of the cell at any time. There was a large hole with a grate over it in the centre of the floor, and the entire room sloped slightly towards it. He tried not to think about that fact.

He leaned his head back against the stone and laughed, long and loud, and thought of Cassidy. "Very clever."

ON SALE NOW FROM ENGEN BOOKS

# THE SIX ELEMENTAL
## ALI HOUSE

The myth of the Six-Elemental is almost seven hundred years old, and the possibility of someone having the power of more than one Element has been thoroughly disproven by science. None of this matters, however, when Kit Tyler receives the power of all six Elements on her twenty-first birthday.

"Blending the worlds of science and mythology, The Six Elemental is a compelling page-turner with a heroine we can all relate to."
Amanda Labonté, author of *Call of the Sea*

Also available: *The Fifth Queen* by Ali House

**JD Ryot** is the reclusive creator of the *Slipstreamers* series from Engen Books. JD is an avid fan of young adult literature and adventure serials. When asked if they had come to this world through a portal themselves, JD Ryot refused to answer. No record of their birth has ever been found... on this world.

---

**Amanda Labonté** is a international bestselling author living in St. John's, Newfoundland, where she gets much of the inspiration for the characters and places about which she writes. She has written seven novels: *Call of the Sea, Drawn to the Tides, Return to the Depths, Supernatural Causes* Volumes 1 & 2, *Lady of Vision*, and, *Mistress of Insight*, all of which are available through Engen Books.

---

**Lauralana Dunne** grew up running around the library stacks of St. John's, Newfoundland, Canada, and has been writing stories for as long as she can remember. She is a die-hard lover of YA Fantasy, and has been known to describe herself as a "Slayer of Imaginary Monsters." Her first novel, *Ashes*, was published in 2020.

---

**Matthew LeDrew** holds an Honours Degree in English from the Memorial University of Newfoundland with a minor in Anthropology. He has served as a jury member for both the 2018 NLBA awards and the 2020 Arts and Letters Awards. He lives in St. John's, Newfoundland.

www.ingramcontent.com/pod-product-compliance
Lightning Source LLC
Chambersburg PA
CBHW051339020726

47501CB00007B/2167